About the author

Jeff Sillett was born and educated in South London at the local Grammar school in Kennington.

A career in football alluded Jeff despite a spell at West Ham United and being chosen for the England under eighteen squad.

Careers in Banking and IT have allowed Jeff to travel the world, but his early days in South London are the backdrop for his first book featuring Bubbles, a London black cab driver, and his rocky road to wealth.

Jeff now lives in the countryside of Buckinghamshire, a far cry from his colourful upbringing in Bermondsey.

BUBBLES

Jeff Sillett

BUBBLES

Vanguard Press

VANGUARD PAPERBACK

A CIP catalogue record for this title is
available from the British Library.

ISBN 978 1 784655 17 4

*Vanguard Press is an imprint of
Pegasus Elliot MacKenzie Publishers Ltd.*
www.pegasuspublishers.com

First Published in 2018

**Vanguard Press
Sheraton House Castle Park
Cambridge England**

Printed & Bound in Great Britain

Dedication

This book is dedicated to my friends and family, and all
the characters I have met who have provided the
inspiration to write this fictitious crime drama.

PART ONE

CHAPTER ONE
BLACKSMITHS ARMS PUB

My dad, Jack, was a typical product of south London back in the day. Left school too early, lived on his wits, loved a drink, a laugh and a sing song. Had money, lost money, had money again, lost it again. He'd been inside for thieving, but only for a couple of years so he wasn't a villain. Well, not in my eyes. He only had two offspring: me, Bubbles (as everyone calls me) and my brother, Todd. Just shy of thirty, he's a couple of years younger than me and lives in Bahrain. He comes back to the UK once in a while, but mainly to see our mum.

I'm a black cab driver in London, and I make a few quid when I decide to graft a bit. My girlfriend, Susie, is the love of my life. We've got no kids and live together in Blackheath. That's mainly thanks to my dad, who stumped up the deposit on the house to get us on the property market, plus some cash from a few moody deals I was involved in around that time. Oh, and I forgot to mention my brother's girlfriend, Kelly. She's an air hostess for Emirates while Todd works in the luxury goods business. They're a great couple, although I think Todd misses the life back home.

Leader of the pack is my mum, Daisy, sixty-nine summers old but still a cracker and the only lady in Dad's life. Unfortunately, he passed away five years ago, but we all miss him every day.

So, that's my family. We squabble like all families but are totally defensive of our own if the enemy want to criticise. Give love to those we hold dear and love us, but make sure that those that don't love us, fear us. That was something my dad always preached, and as a result we don't get many taking the piss.

Now on this particular day, the For Hire light is off in my cab and I'm on my way to the Blacksmiths Arms in Cudham, near Biggin Hill in Kent, to have a glass or two with my dad's best mate, Charlie Simpson. Biggin Hill is famous for the brave pilots who took off from the airfield in their Spitfires to fight in the Battle of Britain in the Second World War.

No doubt Charlie's wife will be lurking, the fearsome Claudette, high maintenance, highly sexed and a danger to any man that's got a dick... oh yeah, that's all of us. Charlie has called a gathering of me, Paul, AKA Wolfy, Pepper and Slippery. I will explain who they all are later, but something must be brewing for us to all have been summoned.

The last to arrive, I receive my customary slagging off from the boys and a sexy gaze over her glasses from the pouting Claudette. I choose to ignore both.

"Hi, Charlie, I could slaughter a Peroni!" I say with an exaggerated dry voice. "Hi, guys, Claudette... Slippery, are you wearing those sunglasses as a Stevie Wonder impersonation?" I always think it best to be on the front foot with these guys, otherwise they will just get stuck in and take the piss.

12

"Very funny, Bubbles. You should be a comedian," retaliates Slippery.

"You never were any good with the banter, were you, Slippery."

"There you go, Bubs, one Peroni."

"Cheers, Charlie."

"Well, chaps, good to see you all. Let's plot over there by the fireplace. We should all get round the table. You okay for a while, Claudette? We won't be long."

Charlie doesn't wait for a reply and Claudette, sat cross-legged on the bar stool with a tiny skirt half way up her arse, doesn't look up as she continues to read her newspaper.

The Blacksmiths Arms is one of those country pubs that's as warm as wallpaper. Brass horseshoes above the bar with a rail to rest your foot and assume the correct position for supping your ale. Fifteen-year-old Axminster carpet on the floor, an open fire with the Guvnor's dog stretched out in front and roast potatoes and a bit of seafood on the bar, free and gratis on Sunday lunchtime... Heaven.

Charlie takes centre stage. "I've pulled you all together because you're all people I can trust. There's a blag coming up and I want to know who's in and who's out. A month from today, so there's a lot to plan. It's high-value merchandise we're knocking off, just a little bit of heavy stuff but no guns. That way, if it goes tits up, the repercussions won't be so bad." He pauses and takes a sip of his drink.

"I need a rider for a motorbike and a driver for a car. Pepper for the bike with Wolfy as the passenger and the main muscle. Bubbles, you can drive the car and Slippery, you're the passenger, quick on your feet to help Wolfy. You'll each get a million, with another half a million six months after the blag. I know the details are sketchy, but I don't want to say much more until you've made your decision... If you're out, leave now, keep your mouth shut and no hard feelings."

Pepper is the first to pipe up. "I can ride a bike, Charlie, but it's been a while."

"We can sort that, Pepper. I have a high-powered BMW you can practise on," says Charlie.

Wolfy is next to speak. "If we're not armed, what are we tooled up with? Knives or what?"

"We can discuss what tools besides a gun are best to frighten the shit out of someone with, but it will only be one, maybe two people we're targeting." After a brief pause, Charlie turns to look at me. "You've only been involved in small jobs, Bubbles. The stakes are high on this one so think long and hard before you give your answer."

It's Wolfy's turn again. "The details are a bit sketchy, but I'm in."

Pepper, lifelong thief, proclaims "I'm in, Charlie."

Slippery, a friend of Pepper since their school days, says "Count me in."

All eyes are on me now. I try not to feel the pressure as I quietly ponder what Susie would say if she knew what was going down here in the Blacksmiths Arms. She knows I'm no angel, but I've never been on a blag where the bounty was one-and-a-half million pounds. All I can think of is how much prison time I'll get if it goes wrong, even if I'm only the driver.

"Yeah, I'm in, Charlie." The words tumble out as if someone else is working my mouth.

Charlie called out to the landlord of the pub. "Another round, 'H', and bring them over. And the same for Claudette." We drink in the Blacksmiths Arms every couple of weeks so 'H' knows us well enough not to get too inquisitive about our conversations. The drinks were delivered and 'H' retreated to the bar at the furthest point away from us and our conversation. Claudette continued to flick through her newspaper but definitely within earshot of all Charlie had said. Even the dog stretched out in front of the unlit fire looked like he had his paws over his ears... Smart dog.

Nothing further was said about the blag that evening, other than Charlie announcing that the next gathering would be in five days' time at his villa in Marbella.

He wanted us to book our flights separately and through different airports. We'd be in Spain for five days and we were to bring our partners along as if it were a holiday. We were not to tell our wives or girlfriends, or anyone else, about the little we knew of the blag, and time would be set aside at the villa to find out more about the caper.

Charlie would pay for all the flights and the women were to be told that it was Charlie's treat as it was Claudette's birthday. I knew she was in her mid-forties as she'd said to me on more than one occasion, "What do you think of my body for a forty-five-year-old? Not bad, aye."

Although by the time we get to Marbella she would probably tell everyone it was her thirty-fifth birthday!

No one other than me had a proper job, so going at short notice was not an issue for them. The girls would just be happy to be away for five days in the sun, all paid for by our host, Charlie Boy. I'd been to Charlie's villa before with my mum and dad when I was a kid, so I remember it well. I think it was the first time I had seen a woman's breast in the flesh and not in a magazine. On this occasion, it was Claudette prancing around the pool topless that filled my virginal eyes... Thank you, Claudette.

The girls had all met before at various gatherings and seemed to get on, although five days under the same Spanish sky may put the cat amongst the pigeons. Wolfy's wife was as hard as her old man and Pepper's other half, Janice, was a London girl who would definitely take no prisoners. It was a clever move by Charlie to have us all at the villa as we could discuss the blag in complete privacy, and inviting the girls was a good cover if any investigating officers should become inquisitive after the event.

I drove back from the pub and my mind was racing as to which merchandise we would be knocking off. Gold, money, diamonds? Just one or two people to hit? Motorbikes and cars? A sick feeling started filling my mouth as I reflected on what I had signed up for.

CHAPTER TWO
MARBELLA

The days flew past and soon Susie and I were packed and ready to leave for Luton airport. Nowhere near Blackheath where we live, but the London airports and Stansted had already been taken by the other couples.

We travelled in Susie's little Kia and parked up in the multi-storey car park at Luton train station, where we hopped on the bus that's laid on to take you to the airport terminal. I'd never travelled with Monarch Airlines before and, to be honest, the smaller airport was a lot less crowded and the people boarding seemed pretty regular. A small crowd of girls, obviously heading to a hen do, were dressed in shorts and cropped t-shirts with the words 'CHLOE'S HENS HOPING TO MEET SPANISH COCKS' on the front... Charming!

We flew to Gibraltar as Charlie's place is midway between Marbella and Gibraltar. Once again, the smaller airport was a welcome change to the mayhem of bustling Malaga airport.

Susie looked gorgeous in her tight white jeans and cappuccino-coloured top, with her blonde hair cut short into her neck. You can take your partner for granted sometimes, but once in a while you look at them as you did the first time you met and fell in love. Beautiful girl.

After a forty-five-minute taxi ride, with the Mediterranean Sea to our right the whole way, we arrived at the gated villa. The sun glinting off the sea sent a tingle through my body... Oh, how I love southern Europe and all it has to offer.

Claudette met us at the gates wearing a sky-blue silk kaftan, matching bikini bottoms and nothing else. My childhood recollections came flooding back and I felt my cheeks colour... Naughty Claudette. We said our hellos to Charlie and dropped our bags off in our room. Charlie had six double bedrooms, all en suite, so plenty of room for all.

We re-emerged for a chilled glass of Sangria. To be honest, I really wanted to take my Susie to bed, as I had wanted to do since Luton airport. We both looked grey compared to our tanned hosts, but with temperatures in the mid-thirties, it wouldn't be long before we would be boasting a Mediterranean glow too.

As always, we were the last to arrive and hugs and kisses were distributed equally to the residents. I don't know why, but some people cannot adapt to new surroundings. In a black outfit that any bouncer on a nightclub door would be happy to wear, hard man Wolfy looked exactly that. Meanwhile, Pepper was wearing a pair of thick-soled shoes best suited to a walking holiday in the Fells. You can take the boy out of south London, but you can't take south London out of the boy.

We all stood around the pool, the girls gathering together to talk. The guys gravitated towards the booze, which would normally be in the kitchen if this were a party in the UK. What with the travelling, it had been a long day for everyone, so we all started to drift off to bed.

Sun, freshly laundered sheets and Susie looking hot are all a recipe for me to act like a dog on heat. I stroked Susie's hair and gently caressed her thighs, feeling the softness of her skin. With Susie's body reacting to my touch, she whispered

"Make love to me, Bub, I want you on top of me."

I was now as hard as a copper's truncheon as I penetrated her wet 'love box', as she liked to call it. Thrusting inside her, she arched her back as I felt her body jolt with her first orgasm. I tried to hold back but when I heard her moan with pleasure it was too late.

"I can feel you throbbing inside me. I love you so much, my darling," she whispered in my ear.

"I love you too, my sweet." Within minutes we were both asleep, the air conditioning whirring above us and cooling our bodies.

Morning came and the sound of a cockerel rang out across the hillside. A peacefulness filled the air, in stark contrast to the sounds of early morning traffic in south London. We showered and slipped on our swimwear and made our way to the kitchen, but not before Susie kissed me hard on the lips and said in a sultry voice, "More of the same tonight, big boy."

"You can count on it," I replied as I could feel myself rising to the occasion… God, I love that girl.

Charlie had arranged a boat trip for the boys from Puerto Banus to the Gibraltar Straits and back so he could talk shop. Claudette had arranged a shopping trip for the girls followed by lunch at the port. All the girls were excited except Bet, Wolfy's wife, who buys her clothes from George at ASDA and thinks Primark is expensive. Wait until she sees the prices at the port.

We boarded the chartered boat at the end of the jetty, which was skippered by Charlie's Spanish friend. Charlie had his own boat years ago and I remembered being on board as a kid, but he sold it a few years back as he rarely took it out. The mooring costs had rocketed, so it didn't make economic sense to keep it.

Charlie could be very logical, sensible and charming as well as hot-headed, violent and a complete arsehole. It just depended what day of the week it was.

Charlie addressed the team, talking freely, as Pedro, our skipper, only spoke Spanish.

"Since we last met I've been busy with the arrangements. We have three weeks before the off, and I'll tell you as much as you need to know at this stage. The merchandise will be transported from Heathrow Airport into the West End by limousine. Inside the limo will be three people, to be confirmed closer the time. One will be an accountant type, with two metallic briefcases handcuffed to his wrists, plus one minder and a driver who will be an ordinary Joe employed by the limo company. Pepper and Wolfy will be following on the bike, while Bubbles and Slippery will be driving in front.

The limo will have a tracking device, so we can agree a time and place to block it with the car. Wolfy and Pepper, you can do your stuff on the accountant and the minder. You need steel cutters, blades, truncheons and pepper spray, all of which will be in the panniers of the bike and in the car.

"The guy with the briefcase is not a heavy, but his minder will be and needs to be put to sleep first. He won't be armed. Bubbles, you need to smash the driver's window before Slippery pepper sprays the driver and does him with the truncheon. We don't want him thinking he can drive off.

"Wolfy and Pepper, put the briefcases in the panniers and make your way to the drop, the whereabouts of which I shall advise you of soon. All go about your business as usual after the blag. No running off at the mouth, no saying nothing to no one. I will contact you in a week's time to arrange the distribution of your equal shares. Any questions?"

"Where do we dump the bike after we've dropped off the cases?" asked Pepper.

"You keep your leathers on and your visor down. Leave it in Shoreditch at the bikers' café, go in for a cuppa and leave out the back. Same for you, Wolfy. Bubbles and Slippery, take the car to the arches in Bermondsey. There are no street cameras so you can make your exit from there. A Ford Focus will be parked there for you with the car keys in the exhaust. Again, quietly go about your business. Give some thought to a plausible alibi for the time you spent on the blag, in case the Old Bill tap you up. Any more questions?" said Charlie, looking around the table.

"Yeah," said Slippery. "We all trust you, Charlie, no question, but the merchandise is left somewhere we don't know. It's a week before you contact us. What's happening during that week?"

"You all have a job to do and so do I. I will be busy that week getting your cash. You will just have to trust me.

Do you trust me, Slippery? Do you trust me, arsehole?" Charlie spat the words out like a Viper.

"Of course, Charlie, of course," said Slippery in a nervous, stuttering response.

"Prick," said Charlie. "Let's have a drink."

The bottles of San Miguel were disappearing at an alarming rate as we drank and reflected on our individual roles and responsibilities. Wolfy was knocking back the Carlos the First brandy, and I could see we were heading for a session.

Wolfy is a hulk of a man with arms the size of my thighs and a bowling ball head sitting on a neck I defy anyone to put two hands around. His missus, Bet, is a solid lump as well. I imagined them having sex and going at each other like rampaging bull elephants.

All the guys are older than me by about ten years, so when we get together there is always talk of blags back in the day, birds and funny stories, most of which have grown legs over the years. Pepper and Slippery, who are the same age and grew up around south London, have the most stories to tell about their past sexual exploits. Pepper had a minicab firm near the Star of India pub in Peckham. His drivers would pick up girls who couldn't pay the fare and would offer sex instead. The girls were encouraged to go to the Star and there would be a lock-in and sex for all.

Another time they picked up a couple of girls in a Kent pub and took them to a local golf course late at night for a shag on the eighteenth green. With their strides around their ankles and mid-thrust, the green was lit up like Crystal Palace as the Old Bill arrived in two squad cars and put their lights on full beam to identify the naughty four ball. They weren't charged, and Pepper always insisted the Old Bill looked like they wanted to join in.

I love Pepper and Slippery. They're like the kid at school who always makes you laugh – naturally funny and cheeky.

I was hitting the vodka and tonics now and Wolfy was leading the chorus of Chas and Dave's song 'Down to Margate' as the boat was closing in on the port. Charlie had a smile on his face but would never lower his guard to be pissed and out of control.

When we disembarked at the jetty, it was a unanimous decision to continue drinking at a local bar. Charlie advised not to go to any of the well-known bars in case any faces from back home recognised us and started asking questions as to why we were all together.

We plotted up in a gaff called Pepe's Tapas Bar. Charlie fancied some Rioja, and four bottles of red wine were put away in record time. We were all on the way to getting wasted, minding our own business and having a laugh, when two birds wandered in with their blokes. The guys and one of the girls was Spanish, but the other bird was English and was showing out to Slippery.

"Where are you from, luv?" asked Slippery from across the bar.

"Stepney originally, but I now commute between Brentwood in Essex and Marbella," she replied.

"Hold up. The Essex girls are here… Lovely," said Slippery with one of his winning smiles.

One of the men said something to Slippery in Spanish, which didn't sound very friendly, and our Essex girl rebuked the guy in Spanish. He replied to her and in the sentence was the word *guapa* (meaning beautiful or gorgeous but which sounds very similar to the English 'whopper'). Well, nobody likes to be called fat, and Slippery was a bit sensitive in that area.

"Who are you calling fat, you Spanish nonce?" screamed Slippery from across the bar. Charlie stepped in and explained in Spanish that there had been a misunderstanding and suggested they jog on. But, fuelled with drink, Slippery had the bit firmly between his teeth and was ready for a row.

Charlie shot him a look and whispered in his ear, "We're trying to keep a low profile while we're in Spain. The last thing we need is the *Guardia Civil* turning up."

When the boys are together, you can bet your life that the evening will end in a fight or a fuck. Charlie suggested we return to the villa for a bite to eat and a drink, and we all agreed.

CHAPTER THREE
CLAUDETTE'S BIRTHDAY

It's day three of the jolly boys' outing, and we're all sat round the pool chilling out. The girls had a good time shopping in the Port, as the bags testified: Prada, Christian Louboutin and Cartier. Even Bet treated herself, though her bag read Poco Loco.

Susie told me that Claudette and Bet had locked horns over the venue for lunch, Claudette heading for a swanky fish restaurant overlooking the fabulous yachts in the harbour, Bet wanting a pizza at Yanks. Claudette won the battle, but it was Bet putting a stake in the ground. She was not used to being told where to eat or being told anything for that matter.

Susie had bonded with Julie, Slippery's girlfriend and Janice's younger sister. Aged thirty-three, she was closer in age to Susie's twenty-seven years. Julie was a worrier, mainly about Slippery staying on the straight and narrow, as trouble seemed to follow him around. Julie was not sure what Slippery did for a living and she knew he had been inside for thieving.

He talked to her a lot about buying and selling cars, and that he and Pepper had a bit of a thing going on with high-performance motors and the profit margins when they sold them were massive. They were, in fact, selling stolen luxury cars to the drug dealers who liked to cruise around their manors in them as a badge of their successful dealings, resprayed with new plates.

Julie's sister Janice is the fun-loving, sex-on-a-stick girlfriend of Pepper. She loves nothing more than to dance, laugh and drink. At a party, Janice is always the one to get the party underway. She's a cracker and never plays away with other blokes, even though Pepper has done a few stretches inside.

Susie asked me what all the boys were talking about when we were together.

"Nothing special," I said in a dismissive manner. "Normal stuff... Football, drink, what we were up to in our private lives... Why?"

"Oh, just something Janice said about Pepper getting ready to court trouble again."

"No. I don't know," I said shaking my head.

If Pepper has been mouthing off about the blag to Janice and Charlie finds out, there will be murder. I went for a cool-down in the pool before she could ask me any more questions.

We all went back to our rooms to shower and change for Claudette's party. Charlie had booked the Mafia table, as he called it, at the *Villa Tiberio* on the golden mile towards the old town of Marbella. An established old Italian restaurant with music and a small dance floor, the gardens are magnificent, with statues and fountains interspersed with a backdrop of beautiful Mediterranean plants and palms. Our table, which was long and seated twelve, was set away from the main body of tables, but close enough that we could look out over all the other diners.

We all looked good, the girls in their new clobber, the guys in Ralph Lauren shirts and light-coloured jeans. I may be biased, but my Susie looked stunning and outshone them all. Why I had not married her yet was beyond me.

We had cocktails in the anteroom surrounded by beautiful statues. All we needed was Caligula and his mistress and we would have the full complement for our table. Why we had a table for twelve when there was only ten of us I couldn't fathom.

Whoever it was, they were running late, and we were heading for the table. We sat boy girl boy girl, the preferred way with mixed diners. Personally, I say put all the guys at one end of the table and all the girls at the other. The guys can have a laugh and the girls can talk hair, weight, clothes and cosmetic surgery... Then we are all happy.

Charlie said the meal was his treat, but we insisted on paying for the champagne we were about to order. The girls had bought birthday presents for Claudette, which they placed on the table for her to open, then the champers was poured. Just as well the girls had the foresight to do that. I hadn't given it a thought.

We raised our glasses and proposed a toast to Claudette and she began to open her gifts, loving all the attention. She was wearing a white stretchy number and her breasts were on show like two prize melons, waiting to be judged 'best in class'. Her dress was so tight that her thong was visible through the thin fabric. I was not sure if she looked like a high-class brass or an ageing film star... Not for me, either way.

The smiles from those on our table told me the mysterious additional diners had just arrived and were making their way to the table.

"What the fuck!?" I said loudly without thinking. It was my brother, Todd and his girlfriend, Kelly. "What are you doing here? When did you arrive? Sit down!"

Charlie's voice rose above the hubbub of diners. "Guys, Claudette and I were great friends of Bubbles' dad, Jack. We had great times together here in Spain, so when we were choosing the guest list, Claudette thought how nice it would be to have Todd and Kelly join us. So, here they are." Slippery filled their glasses with champagne as I stared at them both in disbelief.

"When did you arrive, Todd?" I mumbled.

"This morning. Charlie paid for the tickets and Kelly managed to get us upgraded on Emirates so it was a brilliant trip over."

"Oh. So, where are you staying?"

"At the Marbella Club. I know it's super expensive, but it's only for a few days and the tickets never cost us anything so we thought we would make the most of it."

"You okay, Kelly?" asked Susie. "You look well!"

"Yes, thanks. My job is going well and Todd is settled in his job."

"Oh, that's great," said Susie, and she meant it.

Charlie was back on his feet proposing a toast to his beautiful wife, Claudette. We raised our glasses and said cheers to the birthday girl... Again!

The lobster thermidor was delicious, washed down with more champers. The crème brûlée and chocolate profiteroles fought for popularity, followed by coffee and brandy for the men, and limoncello for the girls. Chocolates were placed on the linen tablecloth and the Italian owner popped over to check that all was good with the meal. Charlie said all was fine and then turned to whisper something in Claudette's ear, which effectively terminated the conversation. He smiled a shark-like grin, revealing white teeth sixty years younger than his weathered face.

Janice took her sister's hand and guided her towards the dance floor. The aged pianist was playing a Boney M song, accompanied by a backing tape. Susie, Kelly, Claudette and, eventually, Bet joined them for a boogie and some fun. We ordered more champagne and brandy and moved seats so all the boys were together.

"I can't believe you're here, Todd," I said quietly. "This is so great and generous and thoughtful of Charlie and Claudette. I haven't seen you for six months, and that was only for an hour when you popped round mum's."

"Well, Bubs, you don't look any different. You're still not as good looking as me, are ya!" Todd said with a cheeky grin. The truth was, I'm not as good looking as Todd. Our faces are the same shape, but those dark 'come to bed eyes' of his set him apart.

"Maybe, but I could always pull the girls better than you."

"In your dreams," he said and grabbed me around the neck, pulled me towards him and planted a kiss on my forehead. Before he met Kelly and we used to go drinking together, the birds would always be after him. He was a cool operator and you never knew who he was shagging... Naughty boy.

I've never been a smoker, but Todd was a twenty-a-day Marlboro Red man, and he had waited long enough for a smoke, so I followed him outside to the gardens where he could light up and we could talk.

"I didn't know you were close to Charlie. It's been five years since you left for Bahrain. I didn't realise he'd stayed in touch."

"Well, not really. He comes out occasionally to see some old friends that he and Dad did some business with. We had dinner together recently. The Middle East is a male domain, and Kelly doesn't get asked to join us. So rather than upset her, I don't tell her if I'm meeting Charlie. He's been good to me since Dad died. It was mainly Dad that put me in the frame for the job I got at the luxury goods company, and I've been promoted recently to logistics director, overseeing the transportation of our most expensive products," Todd said seriously with his work head on.

"Good, good," I said with a nodding head to reaffirm the positive news. Wolfy joined us with a rather large lah-di-dah (cigar) hanging from his mouth and clutching his brandy.

"This is the life, boys: bubbly, birds and a big cigar," purred Wolfy. "These were the days I dreamed of when I was in the nick. I might buy a place out here after the job," he said nonchalantly.

I closed my eyes thinking you pillock, Wolfy, keep your mouth shut. Todd had finished his ciggy, so I took his arm and casually walked him back to the table, leaving Wolfy to gaze up to the sky through the plumes of smoke, totally oblivious to what he had just said.

The evening continued and it was a great night for all. Claudette was disappointed that Charlie had not bought her a birthday cake, but I knew why. He didn't want every punter in the restaurant looking over as a huge cake was delivered to a chorus of 'Happy Birthday to you'. Claudette would have to remain disappointed.

CHAPTER FOUR
TODD

Before we broke for the evening, Susie and I arranged to meet Todd and Kelly at Bikini Beach along the coast towards Estepona. It was a *chiringuito*, a wooden bar/restaurant on the beach specialising in paella and seafood. The Spanish from Madrid love *chiringuitos* when they holiday in the Costa del Sol. The fried fish is typical of the Andalusian area and there is nothing like them inland. We arranged to meet at three in the afternoon – late enough to sleep off our party night and feel peckish.

First to arrive, Todd and Kelly instructed the waiter to position a parasol over them that was large enough to shade the whole table. I don't suppose a suntan was high on their agenda knowing they were returning to the blistering heat of Bahrain.

The girls launched into a conversation about hair, their respective cuts and, randomly, how their house was in Bahrain and ours in Blackheath.

In a hushed voice and half turning his chair away from the girls, Todd asked me if I had plenty of work.

"Not bad," I said. "If you put in a long day, it's still a decent job working for yourself, and I get to work the hours I want. We all moan, but you never see a black cab driver with his arse hanging out of his trousers through lack of money. Although, Uber has arrived on the scene with an app that pinpoints where you are and sends out a request for a taxi. You receive their contact number, the name of the driver and a photograph, and no cash changes hands. Most of the cabbies are saying that black cabs will be a thing of the past in a few years and are looking to get out of the game."

"Black cabs are part of London. I can't see that changing," said Todd. "Are you keeping out of trouble with the girls? I know you've had a wandering eye in the past."

I raised my eyebrows and peered at Todd over the frame of my sunglasses. "I'm a devoted partner to my beloved Susie, a one-woman man who is almost teetotal. My brother, on the other hand, lives with a girlfriend who regularly flies off to destinations all over the world. What is my little brother doing when the cat's away? So, I ask the question back, are you keeping out of trouble?"

We both laughed out loud and Susie turned to give us a quizzical look.

"What are you laughing about? I hope it's not us."

How is it that girls think we are talking about them all the time, when more often than not blokes are not.

"No, darling... Just banter, my sweet."

"You were probably having a laugh about that girl over there on the sunbed with the fake boobs and tattoos," said Susie with a little spite in her voice.

They are incredible, women! Their mind works totally differently to men.

"I'd not even noticed her," said Todd with one of his killer smiles that put Susie off guard... Handsome git. The girls weren't hungry and instead went down to the water's edge to sit on the sand with their feet in the water. Todd looked at me and asked if Charlie had said anything about his last trip to Bahrain.

"No, nothing, why? Should I know something?"

"Has Charlie mentioned anything about a job?"

My heart sank. The thought that my brother might be involved in some way… Mum would go nuts if she knew.

"Okay, Todd, what do you know?" I said with a big brother attitude.

"Well, Charlie said to say nothing to no one, but I figure I can talk to you. Kelly is oblivious to all of this and there is nobody else in Bahrain I can confide in."

"Tell me," I said sharply. Todd moved his chair to face me.

"The company I work for, Aqwad Luxury Goods, are specialists in high-value pearls. These are the types of pearls that when we were kids were featured in TV programmes showing young boys diving deep to the ocean beds on the hunt for oysters. Without oxygen tanks, many didn't survive." He paused and looked round to check no one else was listening. "Well, that illegal pursuit has been resurrected and there is a growing market globally for these unique pearls. They look more like misshapen discoloured teeth, not the symmetrically perfect cultured pearls you see around a woman's neck. The more irregular and misshapen, the more expensive they are," explained Todd.

"So, where do you fit into all this?" I said flatly.

"I am in charge of the logistics for the safe delivery of these pearls around the world. I work for the owner, Theo Aqwad. He was a friend of Dad's and visited

Charlie's boat in Puerto Banus when we were kids. It was Dad that got me the job five years ago. Theo never talks to me about Dad, but Charlie sees him from time to time. When he comes to London, Charlie sets him up with a hooker and tickets for Chelsea. Theo is nuts about Chelsea Football Club."

"Let me stop you there, Todd," I interrupted. "I think I can see where this is leading. We've been briefed to say nothing about the heist of two briefcases full of valuable merchandise, which I am now guessing is pearls?"

"Yes," Todd nodded.

"So, where do you fit in exactly?" I asked again.

"Well, I know the route the briefcases are taking, the two guys accompanying them and the value of the merchandise. Charlie has been planning this with my help for two months."

"Fuck... Dad must have placed you in that job all those years ago waiting for this day to come!"

"I guess so," nodded Todd.

"Is Theo Aqwad in on the scam?" I asked.

"No, I don't think so. He will get his insurance money and we get the pearls. I work for another six months then resign, come back to England and start a new life in London. Kelly and I really miss our families."

"The guys with the merchandise who we are going to hit, are they heavy duty?" I asked, as the sweat leaked out of me from head to toe.

"No, lightweight. One is an accountant who will have the cases handcuffed to his wrists and the minder is in his fifties. He looks heavy but is out of condition and not very brave. I choose them myself."

"You know the police and Theo will come down heavy on you as the possible inside man."

"That's okay, I've managed the logistics of this type of delivery many times successfully. Nothing this high value, but in five years Theo has never had cause to doubt or distrust me. I feel bad about letting him down and ripping him off, as I think he really likes me, but he won't be out of pocket and nobody should be badly hurt."

Todd was making me sweat more, being so bloody chirpy and optimistic as if he didn't have a care in the world. Perhaps he was more like Dad than I was...

At six o'clock we said our farewells and headed back to the villa to pack in readiness for our lunchtime flight home the following day. Todd and Kelly had another two days at the Marbella Club, so Kelly and Claudette had booked a spa treatment for the day we flew home. Which was just as well, as Claudette was sporting what looked like a black eye courtesy of the unpredictable Charlie. Charlie and Todd had planned to kill some time at the hotel having a coffee, awaiting the girls' return and no doubt confirming details of the blag.

CHAPTER FIVE
SQUEEKY BUM TIME

That night when Susie and I got into bed, Susie was saying how much she enjoyed the break in the sun, how wonderful it was to see Todd and Kelly, and how much she missed them both as they lived so far away.

We had both caught the sun and were donning a healthy glow, although mine was more a café tan, just face and arms, whereas Susie had managed to get a beautiful tan save the bikini white bits. She normally goes topless, but not in front of my lecherous mates... No way.

Much to Susie's disappointment, I couldn't satisfy her or myself in bed. I just couldn't get a hard on and believe me Susie did her best. It must have been like trying to crank up an Austin 7 but the engine just wouldn't start! I just couldn't relax; my head was swimming with thoughts of the past ten days. I felt out of my league, like an amateur football team drawn in the FA Cup with a professional club and the realisation during the game that it was being played at too fast a pace to keep up. Smart-talking Bubbles was lost for words and shitting himself.

I went to work the day after we got home, plotting up in the cab outside Goldman Sachs in the City. It was my normal place to start work as their employees often want taken to the airports, which are the best earners for me. I only went to work because I didn't want to be at home staring into space thinking about the blag all the time.

Next thing I hear is someone jumping in the cab.

"Marylebone Station."

"Ok, guv."

He wants to chat, but I can't be arsed.

"I'm catching the train to Chalfont and Latimer. I have a meeting with some finance people," he said with a plumy voice.

I didn't answer, just thought 'bully for you, prick face'. I don't mind taking their money and to be fair many are as good as gold. But some are so far up their own arse, and I could sense this was one who just saw me as a pleb. My lack of response had the desired effect and we continued our journey across London in silence. On arrival I said, "Twenty-five quid, mate – do you want a receipt?"

"Yes, there you are, my man, twenty-five pounds," he replied.

Now, I normally give my business fares a blank receipt so they can fill it in for a larger amount when they submit their expenses. But as nerdy boy never tipped me, I made the receipt out for ten pounds, folded it over and sent him on his way.

I got another fare immediately from a geezer who had just alighted at Marylebone Station. He put his head towards my window and asked.

"Could you take me to Tooley Street, SE1, please? Number fifteen."

"Sure, mate, jump in," I said.

As he settled in the back I looked in my rear-view mirror. He was a big man, tanned almost to the point of looking foreign, but he wasn't. His face looked very familiar, but I couldn't think where I knew him from. He was the first to speak.

"I know you cabbies don't always like going south of the river because you can't always get a fare back."

"True enough, mate, but I'm a south London boy and am always happy to go back home. SE1 is a bit more yuppie these days, so I can always get another fare when I drop you. What takes you to south London?" I asked.

"Oh, my agent's based there and I want to see him about some work he has for me."

Then the penny dropped.

"You're Benny from 'Crossroads'. I knew I recognised you!"

For those who don't know 'Crossroads', it was the first soap opera on television in the UK before 'EastEnders' and 'Corry'. Crossroads was a motel in Birmingham, and Benny was the slow-witted helper there. He was loved by all who watched it.

"Well, my name is Paul, but, yes, I played the part of Benny for many years."

"How brilliant, you were great in that series. You look very tanned. Do you live abroad now?"

"Well, I spend a lot of time in southern Spain with my wife, Sheila. We have an apartment in Marbella."

I nearly crashed the cab! Was he a plant? Did he know something? Or is it just pure coincidence that Benny lives where I have just come back from, where we have been discussing the biggest pearl robbery in the history of thieving...

"Oh, great, I don't know that area, but I hear it's a fabulous place."

I was not going down the road of a cosy chat about my five days in Marbella. We talked some more before I dropped him at the address of his agent. He was funny, articulate and nothing like the Benny he portrayed in Crossroads. It made my day meeting him.

I had only been working a couple of hours but it was enough, and anyway I would be a millionaire in a few weeks so why was I messing about with this crappy job. I drove down Tower Bridge Road, past Manze's pie and mash shop, but I was in no mood to eat so I cracked on down the Old Kent Road past the legendary Thomas A Becket pub. Henry Cooper, the greatest British heavyweight of all time, trained in the upstairs ring there. Cooper, who beat Cassius Clay (Muhammad Ali) with that famous left hook. The bell for the end of the round was rung on the count of eight and Cassius was dragged back to his stool by his American Seconds. The glove was cut, and by the time a new glove was brought to the ring, Cassius had fully recovered and went on to win the fight.

Nobody knows how Cassius Clay's glove had been cut, but we all had a good idea. Henry went on to be knighted and became Sir Henry Cooper. The iconic pub with the training gym and ring is now a Malaysian takeaway or something. Don't get me started on that shit! Oh, it must be progress…

Soon I was into New Cross and on my way to trendy Blackheath Village, home of the Victorian Blackheath murders, and there will be another murder if my mum finds out that both her sons are involved in this caper of ours.

Susie is concerned about me being a bit distant and fed up since our return from Marbella. She was wondering if anything had happened on holiday to upset me or was I getting fed up with her and didn't love her anymore? I reassured her that I loved her more than ever and the only problem was me settling back into work after the high life in Spain. She understood that, but I still couldn't perform in bed. You must have heard the saying 'this has never happened to me before'. Well, in my case, it never had!

CHAPTER SIX
WOMEN POWER

The Spice Girls promoted 'girl power' in the nineties, but it was around long before that. There have been strong women throughout history, including Boadicea, Florence Nightingale, Emily Pankhurst, the lady who was 'not for turning', Margaret Thatcher, and our dearly beloved Queen is no pushover either.

In my world it is my mum, Daisy, who is the rock in our family. Even today at the age of sixty-nine she's a vivacious lady full of elegance and style. Direct and to the point, she doesn't smile as much as she used to. She's not a tactile mum either, but Todd and I love her, and she's the point of reference when we need guidance and support.

I popped round to her place that morning to tell her about Todd and Kelly turning up for Claudette's birthday party in Spain and how well they both looked. Mum was having none of it.

"Why did Todd not tell me he was going to Spain? If he can travel that far he could have continued his journey on to London to see me," she said forcibly. "They're not real friends of Charlie and certainly not that old trollop whose birthday it was. I remember her growing up as a kid. She loved a bloke then and always gave them an eyeful. No bloody class then and no different now."

I put my arm around mum and gave her a squeeze.

"Come on, Mum, I'm sure Todd would have come to see you if he'd had the time, but he had to get back to work. I didn't know he was coming. It was a complete surprise to Susie and me."

"So, who else was there?"

"Wolfy, Pepper, Slippery, me, Todd and Charlie, plus all the girls. We all stayed at Charlie's villa except Todd and Kelly, who stayed at a hotel."

"I don't like you being with that lot. Why can't you be content with Susie's company? Your dad and Charlie were trouble when they were together. You and that crowd spell trouble to me... Who else was there?" She barked through pouted lips.

"Nobody... Like who?"

"I don't know who else Charlie may have invited." She shrugged her shoulders and took her cold, half-finished cup of tea back to the kitchen.

"I want you to tell Todd to call me, I want words with him," Mum called out.

I finished my tea, stuffed the rest of the chocolate Hobnob in my mouth and said my farewells. At no time had Mum asked if we had a good time or made comment that I had a nice colour from the sun. Sometimes you wonder why you bother.

In Wolfy's household, Bet was grilling him about the blag. He'd already spilt half the beans and the other half was tumbling out of his runaway mouth.

"When do you get your money," asked Bet.

"A week or two after the blag," Wolfy replied.

"Is it cash in a suitcase? Is there a divvy up at some out-of-the-way place where everyone gets their readies?

Do you know how difficult it is to shift cash these days?" growled Bet.

"I don't know, luv, we meet again tomorrow to go through the final details and then we hit them on Tuesday."

"You blokes couldn't organise a piss up in a brewery. There is no detail," pointed out Bet.

"For God's sake, woman, we find out tomorrow."

In Pepper's house in Kent, Janice was also on his case.

"You lot are up to something, aren't ya?" she said with a nodding head and arms crossed.

Pepper didn't reply and carried on picking out some winners from the *Racing Post*. There was a card at Romford Dog Track and a mate of his had given him a tip.

"Pepper... I'm talking to you. You lot are up to something, I can tell. Us girls are not daft you know. I have lived with you long enough to know when something is going down. Should I be looking forward to another couple of years visiting you in Belmarsh or some other shithole prison up north? Aren't these cars you and Slippery are selling enough for you?" she shouted at Pepper with her face two inches away from his.

"Okay," said Pepper in an exaggerated whisper. "Charlie is organising a job that, when it comes off, will be big money for you and me."

"I knew it... When it comes off... If it comes off, more like! Are all your little firm in on this?"

"Yes, all of us who were out in Spain except young Todd. We're meeting tomorrow to go through the final arrangements. I think we're nicking diamonds from a courier, but I'm not sure yet."

"Do the girls know about the job?"

"No, nobody knows other than Claudette, who was earwigging at our first meeting. Janice, you cannot say anything about this to anyone. Not even your sister, Julie," pleaded Pepper.

"I want to know chapter and verse tomorrow when you come back from the meet. I don't want you inside again. I couldn't stand it. I want to know every detail to see if your plans for this job are floored. If it looks suspicious, you ain't going on the blag. Do you hear me, John?"

Pepper knew he was in the shit when she called him by his Christian name.

"Yeah, yeah, don't get your knickers in a twist, girl. I've told the boys I'm in, and I'm in!"

With that, Pepper made his way to the front door, shouted out "I'm going to the bookies", slammed the door and left.

CHAPTER SEVEN
FINAL BRIEFING

We all met up at the Blacksmiths Arms for the final briefing. Charlie had booked a room at the back to give us more privacy. It was eleven a.m. on Tuesday, a week away from the blag.

There was only one person in the pub, an old geezer – the guv'nor of the pub's dog, who was stretched out in front of the log fire, despite it being unlit because it was summer.

I ordered a Peroni from 'H', told him to put it on the tab and took the drink to the back room. There was no banter from any of us this morning. We were all wearing our 'game faces' as we were down to the short strokes and the serious stuff.

Charlie stood up and spoke to the group. He had some chalk in his hand and was using the blackboard part of the dartboard to draw the route the limo would be taking and where the hit would take place.

"Right, listen up," said Charlie with a gaze that penetrated the whole team. "Tuesday at six thirty a.m., the courier, minder and driver will be in the limo making their way from Heathrow to a vault in the City to store the merchandise. At approximately seven fifteen to seven thirty, Bubbles and Slippery will be in the car in front of the limo as it makes its way through Vauxhall towards the

City. When the car travels down Lombard Street, which is a fairly narrow road, you stop the car broadside and block their progress.

"Wolfy and Pepper will be following the car on two separate motorbikes, dressed in black leathers and visors. Bub and Slippery, you'll also be wearing leathers and visors to hide your identities.

"You'll be tooled up with truncheons, pepper spray and a blade each. Wolfy and Pepper will also have bolt cutters to remove the briefcases from the courier's wrists.

"It needs to be a proper tear up, lots of noise to keep nosy bystanders away. Smash the limo windows with the truncheons and pepper spray them first. Wolfy, you target the minder, Pepper the courier and Bubbles and Slippery the driver. Try not to use the blades unless absolutely necessary. I don't want a dead body on our hands.

"Bub and Slippery, jump on the back of the bikes, Bub with Wolfy and Slippery with Pepper. Make sure the loot is secured in the panniers and you can race away to the arches in Bermondsey by the Star of India pub.

"There will be a grey Ford Fiesta parked up for you all to make your escape in. Bubbles, you drive and drop the boys off at intervals on route to the David Lloyd Gym at New Cross.

"Bubbles, wear jogging bottoms and a sweatshirt under your leathers. Put the briefcases in the sports holdall in the car. Go to the gym changing room and deposit the cases in your locker. Make sure you have your membership card and key with you on the day. Leave the gym and dump the car near Millwall football ground, go for a beer then call a cab to take you home.

"Wolfy and Pepper, there will be two motorbikes in the pub car park. Have a drive up and down to get used to handling them, take them home with you and use the grey covers in the panniers to cover them from prying eyes. Your leathers are in the other pannier and the helmet in the well under the seat. Bubbles, get two more locker keys cut for me.

"After the blag, go home and chill out. No contact with each other or me. I will contact you in a week's time with your money. No blabbing to anyone about the job, no excessive spending in anticipation of getting your dough. Keep your heads down and your mouths shut. Now, any questions? There's a lot to take in."

I spoke first. "Charlie, what about any DNA on the car, bikes or leathers?"

"Yeah, good one. You will all have gloves on but I will dispose of the vehicles and the leathers. You don't need to concern yourself about DNA as nothing will exist after the blag."

Slippery was next to pipe up. "What's in the briefcases. Diamonds?"

"You don't need to know other than they are of very high value and I am in regular contact with the buyers, who are stomping up the readies for you boys," continued Charlie. "The second instalment of the quarter of a million will be in six months because I want to make sure you all keep your mouths tightly shut." His eyes surveyed our faces for further questions. "Okay, in that case in the box over in the corner you'll find your tools, blades, truncheons, pepper sprays and cutters. There are two holdalls next to the boxes for Slippery and Bubbles containing their leathers, gloves and helmets."

I asked the next question. "You mentioned a tracking device that will be able to pinpoint the limo's exact position. How will that work?"

Charlie replied. "At six a.m. on Tuesday morning we meet at the Heston Services on the M4. There are no cameras there so I'll tell you the make of the limo, colour, registration number and confirm the number of people in the car. At six thirty a.m. I will also confirm that they are on the road and their exact location. They drive past the Heston Services en route so we can top and tail the limo as it approaches. Anything else? All happy?"

A unanimous if unconvincing 'yes' came back from us all.

Charlie had not mentioned pearls or the involvement of my brother, so I kept shtum. No doubt the couriers were instructed to tell Todd when they had arrived safely at London Heathrow and when and where they were in transit. Todd would be passing all the relevant info on to Charlie.

"Okay, boys, the next time we meet will be at six in the Heston Services car park. Try not to contact me before then. If you're worried about something or need to confirm something urgently I'll be at the Blacksmiths Arms between twelve and two on Monday. No mobiles or texts. Speak to me in person." Charlie delivered his words facing the blackboard as he was rubbing out his crude diagram of the limo's journey. Charlie left and I put my box of tricks in the car and returned to the pub for a swift one. Slippery had done the same, but as his belly was up at the bar, he was buying.

"Peroni, Bub?" said Slippery.

"Yeah, nice one," I replied.

"I've never been on a blag that's so meticulously planned, but if I'm nicked I don't even know what I'm nicking," said an exasperated Slippery in hushed tones. "I think it's diamonds but I really have no clue. The Old Bill will wet themselves laughing if we're caught and none of us know. Do you know, Bub?"

"No, I don't. I suppose if he wanted us to know he would have told us."

"What you gonna do with your share, Bub?"

"Nothing for a good few months until the dust settles, but maybe something with Susie. She loves her clothes so maybe a fashion shop selling designer gear. What about you, Slip?"

"We've only got a small cottage in Farningham. We'd like something bigger but in the same area. We like it there," replied Slippery.

We supped up our drinks and made our way home. I'd not had a good drink, laugh or shag in what seemed like forever. I'd be glad when this was all over.

CHAPTER EIGHT
TIMING IS EVERYTHING

I got the locker keys cut for Charlie and arranged to meet him at the Blacksmiths Arms to hand them over, passed a few pleasantries and left. I went through everything in my mind – my role and the areas of risk in the whole plan. My buddies' roles, their weaknesses and whether they would be up for it on the day.

On Monday morning I was taking a shower when Susie popped her head into the cubicle to say Claudette was on the phone and she needed to talk to me urgently. Dripping wet, I stepped out with a towel around my waist and took the mobile.

"Yes, Claudette... Yes, Claudette," was all I said. I finished and deleted the call.

"What's happened?" said Susie.

"It's Charlie, he's had a turn and she wants me to go round there while they wait for the doctor."

"Oh, my God! Is it a heart attack?"

"Could be, I'll shoot round there and keep you posted."

"Would you like me to come to see if I can help in any way," Susie said caringly, her hand rubbing my arm.

"No thanks, darling. Now, I must get ready to go."

What I told Susie was utter bullshit. Claudette said there was a major problem regarding tomorrow and

Charlie wanted to see me *now* at the Blacksmiths Arms, and to pick up Slippery on the way. I called Slippery and told him there was a problem and I would be at his place in half an hour. "Be ready to leave straight away."

Slippery and I arrived at the Blacksmiths Arms within an hour. The pub was closed but 'H' let us in, nodded and said, "Out the back."

The room stank of cigarettes and stale ale from the previous evening's lock-in. The locals must have been smoking. I was surprised to see Charlie, Claudette and Bet all standing by the bar drinking coffee and staring at us as we came through the door.

"What's happened, Charlie?" I demanded.

"It's Wolfy and Pepper. The Old Bill picked them up at five this morning," said Charlie with a snarl on his face.

I wasn't sure if I should talk about the blag in front of Bet, but what the heck.

"How the fuck did they find out about the job?"

"They haven't! There was a job done in Hatton Garden over the weekend, safety deposit boxes. The Old Bill don't have a clue who did it and are just rounding up faces with prison records for thieving who may have been involved.

"Wolfy's brief told Bet they would be keeping them at the station nick for forty-eight hours while they carry out their investigations."

"Incredible… Timing is everything. So, what now. Is it all off?" I asked, aghast.

"It could be, but Claudette has made a proposition that her and Bet take the places of Wolfy and Pepper. They both know the plans, despite me saying to keep shtum. Bet used to run with the Hells Angels and she knows how to ride a high-performance bike. Claudette drives the quad bike at home, so with a bit of practice this afternoon she could be okay by the morning."

"Oh, Charlie, this is ridiculous," pleaded Slippery. "No disrespect to the girls, but women on a blag... And what about the muscle without the boys!"

"I have whacked a few blokes in my time and I am sure Claudette can handle herself," said an unsmiling Bet.

"What about you coming on the blag, Charlie?" I suggested.

"No way. I'm the only one who knows our inside man and the buyer. I need to be totally clean on this one. I can't run the risk of the Old Bill getting a whiff of me when they close the net on who could be involved."

"Well, Pepper and Wolfy have the perfect alibi as they are both inside, and the girls don't have a record with the Old Bill. Neither do I, so if all goes to plan we might be in a better position," I said with some optimism.

Charlie was warming to the situation as tomorrow would be our only bite of the cherry for the merchandise – and the enormous sum of money.

"Bet, you could ride one bike and Slippery you could ride the other," said a very animated Charlie.

"I can ride a bike," said Slippery with as much enthusiasm as a turkey has for Christmas.

"Claudette, you could go in the car with Bubbles. Slippery and Bubbles, you have to take care of the strong-arm stuff and cutting the cuffs off the accountant. Girls, you use the pepper spray and the truncheons if you can. No talking. We don't want them to know that two of our team are women. Bubbles and Slippery, I'll rely on you for a noisy tear up. Frighten the shit out of them," said an excited Charlie.

All I could think of was that I had been promoted from driver to the strong-arm leader of a gang of four, two of whom were women. My brother, a thousand miles away, was our inside man. Charlie (Lord fucking Dunabunk) was directing operations from way behind the front line, sipping tea and getting ready to count his dough. You couldn't write the script, unless it was a comedy.

I considered pulling out, but we were less than twenty-four hours away from a job valued at… Well, I wasn't sure how much the job was worth. What a fucking mess.

Slippery began to plead with Charlie. "I know a few geezers who could come in at short notice for this type of money. It would be better than two women. No disrespect, girls."

"Fuck off, Slippery," said Bet. "Oh, no disrespect, boys."

I almost laughed, but Charlie let Slippery have both barrels.

"I don't want any old lags who are mates of yours and who have done time. They'll have the Old Bill crawling all over them. I want people I can trust and that's the girls. They've been part of the firm since the time they hooked up with us and they've put up with us over the years. I would back Bet and Claudette to outperform any of your arsehole mates," said bully boy Charlie.

"Okay, Charlie, wind your neck in, I was just saying…"

"Well, don't 'just say'," Charlie interrupted.

Charlie went through the whole plan for the girls' benefit and as a refresh for me and the verbally abused Slippery. Bet took a call on her mobile from Wolfy's brief. He was still banged up and initial investigations couldn't pin anything on him for the Hatton Garden robbery, which by now had gone viral. Everyone was talking about it, particularly as the Old Bill had received a call about someone being on the premises but had failed to follow it up… Crazy.

In the pubs they were saying how it was an old school replica of a job done years ago. No one had been hurt so the public's attitude was to hope they got away with it… Time would tell.

As far as our old school blag, we were as ready as we could ever be. I picked the car up, left it in a lock-up close to home and arranged to pick Claudette up at five a.m. the following morning. None of us would sleep much between now and then.

That night Susie and I made love, which was tender and loving. If all went well, I would propose to Susie afterwards. If it didn't that could be my last shag for a long while.

CHAPTER NINE
D-DAY

At five a.m. on the dot, Claudette climbed into the car clad in her leathers with her visor under her arm, sunglasses on, looking like a Bond girl. We looked an odd couple dressed in our biking leathers but in a car.

"Exciting isn't it, Bubbles," said a pouting Claudette.

"Well, it certainly gets the adrenaline pumping," I replied.

"Sure does," she said, as she reached across and gave my wedding tackle a squeeze.

"We've got plenty of time to pull over for a cuddle… Give us a kiss," she demanded.

"Behave yourself, Claudette, and concentrate on the job. We can't afford any mistakes and you need to get your game face on for when the violence starts. This ain't a movie, its fucking scary when it kicks off. So, leave me alone and focus. And take those fucking sunglasses off."

"Yes, sir. How forceful my young love has become," she said in a Yoda from *Star Wars* voice. She was a funny fucker and nothing phased her.

We made our way to the meet at the Heston Services car park for our final briefing. Charlie looked anxious, as did we all – except for Claudette, who had a playful smile on her face. Charlie caught a glimpse of her and snarled at her.

"Shape up, Claudette. This ain't a fucking shopping trip. Don't be our weak link. Do you hear me?" I could see another black eye coming for Claudette if she didn't change her attitude soon. Her face changed and a more competitive attitude returned. Order was resumed.

"Bubbles, there's a new place for the hit: Holborn Circus. You block the car broadside across the road. Do it just after Chancery Lane tube station. There are four exits at Holborn Circus roundabout. Choose the one that takes you to Bermondsey. No half-hearted blows. It will give them the chance to retaliate. Hit 'em and hit 'em hard. The limo is picking them up now and will be leaving Heathrow in five minutes. Slippery and Bet, drive in single file at a safe distance behind the limo. No speeding and drawing attention to yourself."

"Do we need to pay the London congestion charge?" asked Slippery.

Aghast, Charlie replied. "Let me get my credit card out and pay for that now under my name... You fucking dipstick. The motorbikes are nicked. Shall I tax and insure them as well? If you had a brain you could be dangerous... Arsehole."

We all fell about laughing, more through nervous energy than anything else.

The game was on. We boarded our vehicles as Charlie took a call (from my brother presumably) to find out the limo's exact location. The sound of good luck being wished by all quietly echoed around the car park. We took our positions on the road and within fifteen minutes our car was in position, about four motors ahead of the limo. So far, so good. I had a sick feeling in the pit of my stomach like I hadn't eaten for a week and I could feel the bile filling my mouth. I think it's known as fear.

The pepper spray and truncheons were on the floor of the car. "Claudette, you spray the driver in the face first and I'll target the heavy with my truncheon. If anyone gets out of the car, hit them repeatedly as hard as you can. Give them everything you've got. The other two have got the cutters so they can focus on the courier."

I turned towards Claudette as she nodded in recognition of the instructions and placed her helmet on her head. She looked terrified.

The limo was just making its way past the old Prudential building, with the brickwork reflecting the beautiful pink of the early morning sunlight. We were directly in front of the limo now and I slammed on the brakes to bring the car broadside. I leapt out of the car with Claudette running behind in my slipstream. The two motorbikes were strewn across the road, abandoned by Bet and Slippery, as we all raced towards the limo.

Screaming like a banshee, I came to a halt by the driver's door and hit the window with the truncheon, only to see the truncheon bounce off. I tried again and the same thing happened. Slippery saw what was going on and came over with the bolt cutters, which he used to demolish the driver's window and the front screen window.

Claudette sprayed the driver in the face as he reached to open the door. His screaming filled the air as he got out of the car and ran round in circles holding his face. As he vacated the limo, I ran round and floored him with the truncheon. The blow to the back of his head ensured he was out like a light.

Slippery was in combat with the heavy. He was desperately trying to get out of the car to use his strength in the fight, but Slippery kept him pinned down in the car. He took out his blade and slashed him across his face. The claret sprayed everywhere and Slippery moved in to finish the job with three blows to the head with the truncheon. The big man slumped unconscious in a heap on the back seat.

Bet was great. She had the courier trembling in his seat, next to the stricken heavy, just by putting her finger to her lips to say quiet and nothing will happen to you.

Slippery cut the chains from the accountant's wrist, which were securing the two silver briefcases, and passed the cases to Bet, who raced back to the bike to put them in the panniers.

A small crowd had gathered, but they stayed well back. I did notice at least one bystander recording events on his mobile phone, but you would have great difficulty describing any of the leather-clad attackers, who were all wearing crash helmets.

We mounted the bikes and sped off towards the City. As we did, I looked over my shoulder and saw some of the public moving forward to help the injured.

The whole robbery must have taken no more than five to ten minutes. It was as if the whole thing had happened in slow motion. It had gone like clockwork, no fatalities on their side and not a scratch on any of us. We were making our way to the arches to dump our bikes and leathers and go our separate ways. I put the cases into my sports bag and, wearing my tracksuit bottoms, sweatshirt and trainers, I made my way to the gym to deposit the cases into my locker.

You expect a blag like this to involve moving gold bars or bundles of money, but we had seen nothing other than two shiny briefcases. For the first time, a doubt entered my head. Were the valuables inside the cases? Could it be a decoy trip with empty cases while another courier, travelling on the London Underground, delivered the real stuff? It has been done before – many times before.

Charlie was the only one who would see the contents of those two cases and knew their value. Why would it be two weeks before we saw any cash? Was my cut of a million plus half a million in six months enough? Never once had I doubted Charlie to do the right thing, but here I was with all these thoughts playing havoc with my brain.

As I approached the gym I saw a figure half hidden in the shadows peering out. Was it Charlie? I carried on walking, half turning to see if I was being followed. What I did next I hadn't planned. What possessed me to do it I have no idea.

As I reached the gym reception, I said to the guy, "Can I rent a second locker?"

"Sure, Bubbles, here you go." He handed me a key for locker number 333. "You signed a direct debit so we can adjust the amount to cover the two lockers."

"Thanks, mate," I replied

So that was it. I put the cases in the newly acquired locker and fucked off home.

CHAPTER TEN
BAD TEETH

That evening I showered, shaved, put on my best clobber and took Susie out to our favourite restaurant, *Le Pont de La Tour*, under the shadows of Tower Bridge. This has been a favourite of ours for years and it held many memories for me both as a couple and on my own.

I remember one Friday evening meeting my best mate, Clarkie, from my school days for a modest quencher after a week of graft. They had vodka on show with gold flakes floating in the bottle. The barman noticed our intrigue and poured us a glass each on the house for us to try before asking if we'd tried the vodka with caramel. Without waiting for a reply he poured another couple in chilled glasses fresh from the fridge and said 'on the house'.

Clarkie and I looked at each other, then back at the barman, who said, "It's my last night working here. I've seen you here before. Have what you want, you don't need to pay. I couldn't care less."

Never one to look a gift horse in the mouth, we made a professional job of demolishing as much free vodka as we could get down our necks.

We somehow managed to drive to our respective homes, totally pissed. Halfway there, my stomach reminded me that I hadn't eaten since breakfast and I was starving. I was so hungry I picked up a chicken curry and decided to eat it whilst driving, but the only implement I could find in the cab was a golf pitch repairer – ask your golf friends – which I used to shovel the curry into my mouth. Well, some of it. I got home having miraculously made it without crashing and somehow finishing the curry. I stepped out of the cab to see my white shirt with more stains than a butcher's apron, while Clarkie slept in the bath that night, fully clothed. Everything makes perfect sense when you're pissed.

However, this night would be different. It was a special night. With Susie looking ever more beautiful once we were settled and had a flute full of bubbly, I gently took her hand and gracefully went down on one knee. With a gleaming smile on my face, I asked the love of my life to marry me, and without hesitation she nodded a tearful 'yes'. Thank God! Although I had no ring to put on her finger, we both stood up from the table, I took her in my arms and we kissed for so long that the other diners broke into applause. Susie was so happy she couldn't wait to call her mum and tell her the news. We went home, made love and I fell even more in love with her.

I suggested we marry and honeymoon in Bahrain and Todd could be my best man. Susie was jumping on the bed, screaming with delight. It was the happiest I'd ever seen her.

When morning came I had to come to terms with what I had done after the blag, and the strange decision to change the locker. Radio silence was maintained by the team as agreed. The press was full of the blag, which fought for column inches with the Hatton Garden robbery.

Wolfy and Pepper had been released as the police had no evidence to link them to that robbery, and no one had knocked on my door. I had not set foot outside my door after the evening at *Le Pont*.

I needed to speak to Charlie, but before that I needed to chat with my brother, Todd, to try and make sense of my last-minute actions. I drove to Shoreditch, to the café for black cab drivers where there is a payphone. You could always get a cup of tea and a cooked breakfast there twenty-four/seven. It was never too crowded and the phone was near the entrance so nobody could earwig.

I dialled the number in Bahrain.

"How are you, Todd? It's Bubbles."

"Yeah, good, mate, you okay? Can you talk freely?"

"Yes, no problem." I said

"Hang on, let me just close my office door."

He returned. "Have the Old Bill called on you?" I asked.

"Yes, I was interviewed by the local Bahrain police along with Theo Aqwad. They said they think that the gang in London might have used inside information. My assistant manager was the main interrogation target and I think he took a few slaps. They were interested in my trip to Europe, but as it was Spain and not London, they soon lost interest. What about everyone else, Bub, has anyone been in for questioning?" Todd calmly asked.

"Yes, but before our blag and in connection with the Hatton Garden job. Wolfy and Pepper were hauled into the nick for forty-eight hours of questioning the day before our job, which meant that Claudette and Bet took their place. But they did great, Todd, just great... Tell me, how much are the pearls worth on the open market, what is your cut, and what are the combinations for the briefcases?"

"Well, Bamber Gascoigne, retail is forty million, but to a moody fence buyer, twenty to twenty-five million. The codes are 1357 and 1458. My cut is one million and a further half a million in six months' time, if all is well. What do you mean, what are the codes? Hasn't Charlie opened the cases yet?"

"No, I've got the cases. I don't know why, but at the last minute I didn't want to give them up to Charlie so I have them stashed somewhere safe. By my maths, if five of us are getting one-and-a-half million pounds, that totals seven and a half million. Why should he be getting fifteen million plus? He wasn't even on the job – it wouldn't have worked without you. You and I could have pulled this caper off on our own!"

"Yes, but we didn't. It was Charlie's plan from day one, so it's maybe right that he gets the lion's share," said an unconvinced Todd.

"I don't know about that. Dad worked this blag out years ago and got you the job with Theo. Do you think Theo is in on it?" I asked.

"No, I don't. He's worried sick. He has daily meetings with the insurance people. The Old Bill are on his case, and with all that he's going through I remain his confidante. What will you do with the pearls? You don't have the contacts to fence this sum of money. Charlie has all that worked out," pleaded Todd.

"I don't care, I just feel like we are being ripped off. I want a bigger share and so should you," I said emphatically.

"What leverage do you have over Charlie to get a bigger cut?" Asked Todd.

"I have the pearls, he doesn't. That's my leverage."

"He's not a man to be messed with, Bubbles. Be careful how you play this. But whatever you decide your cut should be, demand the same for me... Fuck it... Do you really think Dad put me up for this job just for the blag, Bub?"

"Yes, I do, and Dad would have given us equal shares, not a poxy million. I can't even see Charlie giving us the additional half a million in six months' time. Four million for all the team seems a better number. and I shall be seeing Charlie today to tell him."

"I'm in, Bubs, you can count on me. Just let me know what I can do to help."

"Well, there is one thing before I hang up. I've asked Susie to marry me and I would like you to be my best man. We want to marry and honeymoon in Bahrain."

"Fantastic... About bloody time. Great news, Bub. I'll be delighted to accept your invitation. This telephone line is private and safe and calls from you to me could be about the wedding if the Old Bill happen to discover it. Listen, I know you can handle yourself, Bub, but be careful with Charlie," Todd said with warmth in his voice.

"Will do, mate. If you need to get a message to me, do it through Mum. I'm on my way there now to tell her the news about me and Susie."

"Okay, and let me know the date for the wedding. Kelly will be so pleased."

With that, I ended the call and jumped in the cab to see Mum.

I arrived at her house just before lunch. The house had its own unique smell of laundry and home-baked cooking. I loved it... It was home.

She'd read about the job in the tabloids and knew that the merchandise had come from Todd's firm. Charlie had also called her multiple times asking if she had seen me because he wanted to speak to me... I bet he did.

Mum knew straight away the connection. She would hate the idea of her boys being involved and what the outcome would be for us if we got rumbled. I quickly turned the conversation towards the wedding news. She was delighted and thought that Susie was a lovely girl for me to marry. I wonder if Susie's parents would feel the same about me as their daughter's catch, especially if they ever found out about my involvement in the robbery.

Mum grilled me about the robbery. Who was involved and were the police on anyone's case? She asked lots of questions about Charlie and Todd, and if Theo was clued up on the job. I answered her with an economy of detail but told her that I had the pearls safely tucked away.

Mum had spent a lifetime with Dad ducking and diving around all sorts of illegal activities, so she was no shrinking violet when it came to trouble.

"You should involve me when you talk to Charlie," said Mum with a face on her I remembered from when I was in trouble at school.

"No, I'm not taking my mum along to a meeting like this. I can handle Charlie," I said flatly.

"I have more on Charlie Watson than you know. We go back a long way and he doesn't frighten me. He might knock that slapper wife of his around, but I can give as good as I get."

"Mum, I don't think anyone frightens you, but you might frighten a few yourself. You're still not coming though."

I got up from what was Dad's old armchair, kissed Mum on the forehead, said my goodbyes and got back in the cab as my next stop was the gym to inspect the merchandise.

As I approached I saw Ernie Small, one of Charlie's men, parked up opposite the gym. He was so engrossed with the remaining contents of his crisp packet that he didn't notice me slip in through the gym door. I made my way to the locker room and opened door number 333. The room was empty, and there were no cameras for obvious reasons. I rolled the numbers in the tumblers on each case and slowly opened each of them, rotating my head like a piano stall, looking around for unwanted visitors.

Inside the suitcases were hundreds of pearls in cellophane bags, with fifty or so pearls per bag. The shade of discoloured teeth, they were quite irregular in shape – not at all like the smooth, white, perfectly round cultured or glass pearls that I was familiar with. They were exactly as Todd had described them.

To my eyes they were unattractive, but nevertheless they were worth shit loads of money. I returned them to the cases and put them back in the locker after resetting the tumblers to random settings. I slid out of the gym without the dopey Ernie Small even knowing I had been there.

My next telephone call was to Charlie.

"Hi, Charlie, it's me. We need to talk," I said firmly.

"You fucking bet we do. Where are you, you cunt?" he yelled.

"I'll meet you in the old snooker club in Peckham High Street. It's now a Costa Coffee. Two o'clock," and I hung up. I wanted it to be the venue of my choice. My territory. I'd watched my dad play snooker there for hours when I was a boy and I needed a bit of his karma to help me through this.

CHAPTER ELEVEN
NEGOTIATIONS

I had just enough time to pop into Manze's at the top of Peckham High Street for some pie and mash. I hadn't eaten since my *fruits de mer* at *Le Pont de la Tour*, and the emptiness in my stomach wouldn't let me pass the famous Cockney eating house.

The cutlery was still the same: oversized spoons and heavy forks, with Guy's Hospital engraved on the handles. The diners never change, and it was good to see young mums introducing their nippers to the gastronomic delights of the 'green liquor' that is poured over the pies and mashed potato, originally made from the juice of the eels, with parsley mixed in. A filling meal that was a staple diet for the poor of London, you either hate this cheap meal or love it and will defend your local pie and mash shop as the best in London.

Following my double pie, double mash and liquor I left with a contented feeling, ready to do battle with Charlie, who was already at a table with a cup of tea in front of him and a face like a smacked arse. Charlie spoke first as I took my place opposite him.

"What the fuck are you playing at, you nonce... Where are the cases?"

"Calm down, Charlie, they're safe. I just want to have a chat with you about their value and the split for me and the boys."

"Oh, you do, do ya? Well, boy, your split was nothing until I came along and set this up for you muppets," said Charlie through gritted teeth. "The job went like clockwork, even with a couple of tarts in the team. You will be a million and a half better off thanks to me, and don't you forget it." He poked my chest hard with his finger to reinforce the point and release some of his aggression.

"Charlie, if I take the million and a half and buy a decent house, it doesn't change my life. I'm back in the black cab and life goes on as before. You, on the other hand, could have creamed off fifteen to twenty million for you and your good lady, and that would be life changing. It was my dad's foresight to put Todd in the job in Bahrain, plus his inside information and my leadership during the actual raid, that got us over the line. You, Charlie, were not even there! So why you think you're entitled to so much and me and Todd so little beats me."

"Oh, so, you and Todd, is it? Both trying to shaft me."

"Shaft you! That's rich when we are getting such a small cut of the spoils while taking all the risks."

There was an awkward silence as Charlie eventually sneered, "Where are the cases?"

"All in good time… A tea please, luv," I said to the waitress as she passed by our table, giving me a gorgeous smile. "Okay, Charlie, this is the revised plan. I go with you to meet and liaise with the fence who is buying the stuff. I'll keep the merchandise in my possession until the transaction is completed to my satisfaction and all the funds are with me. The split will then be decided by me and Todd."

"Who do you think you and your bastard brother are, trying to rip me off," Charlie screamed.

"*You* were ripping *us* off, Charlie, but we will be fair with your split and the boys will get their deserved cut as well."

"Just like your old man, he was a greedy fucker."

With that I stood up and pushed a tenner into the waitress' hand as she put the tea on the table.

"Charlie, you've bad mouthed everyone who is dear to me so I'm off. You call me when the meet is arranged with the fence and don't think you can bully me. I'm twenty-odd years younger than you, in better shape and I could take you in a straightener. Don't come to my house and don't talk to Todd. You deal with me and just me. And if you ever slag off my family again, I will rip your fucking head off."

We were locked in a stare for what seemed like an eternity before I made my way to the exit. The waitress offered me my change. "Keep it," I told her.

"Thank you, handsome... You can come again whenever you want," she said with a seductive look on her pouting face.

Outside I took a deep breath and marched to the cab, which was still parked in a side road by the pie and mash shop. I'd surprised myself with the way I had handled Charlie, and I was pleased with how I had handled the blag too. Maybe I had found my forte and was custom built to be a villain! It's all in the breeding, you know.

CHAPTER TWELVE
THE FAMILY

Leaving Charlie to stew in his own juices and await the repercussions, I had a new agenda. I still had rings to buy so I picked up Susie in the cab and we made our way across town to Hatton Garden to have our engagement and wedding rings made.

Isaac Goldberg's family had been in the jewellery business in this area for generations. We passed through the double security doors, where we found Isaac at his workbench awaiting our arrival. After the introductions, Susie and I sat across from the heavily scored lump of oak, which was Isaac's daily place of work, as it has been for his ancestors over the decades.

Whilst Susie and Isaac designed our rings, my mind wandered to a story my dad had once told me about a cleaner in Hatton Garden who had a clientele of mainly manufacturing jewellers. He would vacuum around the work benches, between the cracks in floorboards and over the carpets then go home to sieve the dust bags for shavings of gold and silver.

Within ten years, the cleaner had retired early to live the good life in a villa in Spain, all from the proceeds of the gold and silver he had acquired over the years. How simple and sort of legal. Exactly the same thing was being done in Birmingham. As the turners stood at their lathes shaving the gold and silver into ornaments or bands of gold, they would secrete the filings in their turn-up trousers – this was the era they were introduced – march past security and tip out their daily bounty when they got home.

With the drawings of the rings complete and the deposit handed over, we left the building. My neck was like a piano stool – I couldn't relax thinking someone might be following me. We were in Greville Street so we stopped for lunch at the Bleeding Heart restaurant. Susie and I reminisced over our life together so far and the happy times we've shared. We sat outside and ate tuna niçoise accompanied by a large glass of sauvignon blanc as the weather was cool but sunny.

The site of the Bleeding Heart is famous for the horrific death of Lady Elizabeth Hatton. It was the site of a grand ball, held on twenty-sixth January 1626, where the young and beautiful, including Lady Hatton, danced the night away. A European ambassador, believed to be from Spain, danced with Lady Hatton and escorted her through the doors into the garden, leaving the guests to gossip.

The pair never returned and, in the morning, Lady Hatton's dismembered body was discovered in the cobbled courtyard in Bleeding Heart Yard, yet her heart was still pumping blood. The ambassador was described as being hunchbacked with a clawed right hand, and the guests were left pondering whether the figure dancing with her was the Devil himself. The event was recorded in *Chaucer's Tales*.

Even though Susie and I couldn't have been happier, I was still feeling edgy and had a constant feeling of being watched – maybe by the Old Bill, but more likely one of Charlie's goons. I wasn't in fear of my life because if I was killed, no one would know where the pearls were hidden. More likely I was just getting a bit paranoid.

We finished our meal with an espresso followed by a chilled glass of limoncello, which Susie had acquired a taste for in Marbella. We also agreed a date for the wedding in Bahrain in three months' time.

Susie wanted to see her mum and tell her the good news, so I dropped her off at her house without going in. I told Susie that I ought to get back to work and earn some money for the big day, but the truth was I needed some thinking time as the boys would be expecting their share of the loot in ten days' time.

I stopped at a local park and sat on a bench to plan my next step. Divide and conquer was the best strategy, I decided. I needed the team behind me as a defence against Charlie. If I didn't do that, he would certainly turn them against me, telling them I had kept the loot for myself and cut them out. We had the 'no contact for two weeks' mandate still in place, and I hoped that this was still the case and Charlie had not got to them.

I targeted Pepper and Slippery first as I knew Wolfy was a loyal soldier to Charlie. I got word to them both to meet me in the Bleeding Heart at six that evening. I booked the 'office table' where you could close the door and not be overheard and made it clear to tell no one about our meeting – not the girls, not Wolfy and definitely not Charlie. It was important to come alone and be on time.

I arrived a little early as the waiters were transitioning from the lunchtime to evening sitting and explained that we were not looking to eat until later. Instead, I asked them to put bottles of red and white wine, still and sparkling water on the table. I'd booked under the name Smart, which is what I needed to be to pull this off. The boys arrived looking pensive. I sat them down, poured them a drink and closed the door to the private dining room.

"Okay, guys, straight to the point. Have you told anyone about coming here, and do you think you were followed?" They both shook their heads without comment. "Charlie is trying to rip us off... we each get one million pounds with the promise of a further half a million in six months. The contents of the two cases have a value of twenty to twenty-five million plus. That means a possible twenty million for Charlie, who never even came on the blag." Silence filled the air as the boys took in the sums.

Pepper was the first to respond. "The bastard. It was his idea for the blag but fuck me. The greedy shit."

Slippery continued. "I've spent that million a hundred times over in my mind and the money goes nowhere. Paying debts, a holiday, maybe an extension on the house and then back to the same old same old."

Slippery had the bit between his teeth now. "Let's get him and torture him, find out where the money is and then top him."

"Steady, boys," I said in dismay, although this was exactly the reaction I wanted.

"How did you find out it was worth twenty-five million?" enquired Pepper.

"Let me explain all," I said while refreshing the glasses.

"Five years ago my dad put Todd into a key position at the Luxury Goods Company in Bahrain with the long-term plan to carry out this robbery. Even Todd, the inside man, who chose the lightweight muppets in the limo, the route and the timings, and tracked their movements, still only gets the same as us."

"Todd was our inside man... So that's why he was in Marbella. He set up the whole thing," said Pepper as his eyes looked up towards the ceiling, as though he were thinking out loud.

"Yes," I restated, to stress the point. "He selected the overaged, overweight security heavy, the weak courier who gave up without a fight and the limo company. Plus he dictated their route."

"We've got to get our hands on that money," said Slippery. "I'm not having this piss take from Charlie. I haven't slept wondering when the Old Bill will be knocking on my door and I haven't set foot outside the house since the blag, until now. I'm even putting my bets on at the bookies over the phone, while he sits in his fucking ivory tower. He was nowhere near the blag and has no chance of the Bill feeling his collar. I'm sure he's sleeping easy in his bed counting his fucking millions."

"Well, here's the rub. Charlie isn't counting his millions, nor threading pearls onto a never-ending necklace, because I have the pearls. I never put them in the agreed place for Charlie to collect." There was stunned silence, so I continued.

"I had a sixth sense we were being turned over, so I have them safely stored. I've met Charlie and told him I want to be part of the negotiations with the fence who is buying the pearls. I want to know how much money he's offering and when and how we get the money. Then I will give fair and equal shares for all, and that is not a poxy million each."

"Where are the pearls?" asked Pepper directly.

"Safe, Pepper. It's better you don't know in case Charlie or any of his cronies or the Old Bill get heavy. You can trust me, guys. I wouldn't be telling you all this if I was planning to screw you. I would just fuck off with the loot for myself and say nothing." Once again, silence filled the air as I refreshed the glasses.

"We have to trust you, Bubs. So how much do we get under our new boss, Bubbles," said Slippery with a hint of sarcasm.

"Four million each, across the board. You, Pepper, Wolfy Todd, me and Charlie."

"Charlie?" Exclaimed Slippery "He doesn't deserve a penny!"

Pepper answered for me. He always did have more brain cells than Slippery. "You give Charlie nothing and what stops him going to the Old Bill and grassing us up or topping us while we're asleep in our beds with our newfound wealth. We have to give him a decent share, even if it goes to Claudette, who was at least on the job."

Slippery grimaced but could see the logic. "Look, guys, this job has gone like a dream. No major casualties, none of us clocked at the scene of the crime, no Old Bill on our case, and we are sitting on the loot. Let's not spoil it now. We need to be solid, together and smart, particularly with Charlie. But I need your backing if things get awkward."

"What about Wolfy. Why isn't he hearing all this?" said Slippery, checking the empty bottles for any dregs he could drink.

"Wolfy is a great ally of Charlie's and he's loyal. He will support Charlie in a confrontation. The main motivation for us all is the money, and Wolfy is no exception, but he needs to be handled differently. Also, if I had invited him to this gathering I couldn't guarantee he wouldn't pick up the phone and tell Charlie. I'll deal with Wolfy, but it's important that we three and Todd are united on this. I know Todd is with me, so can I count on you to stand firm and back me against Charlie if the going gets rough? It's worth four million pounds to you so what do you say?"

"I'm in," said Pepper.

"I just want to top Charlie," said Slippery.

"I'll take that as a yes. Now, let's get some more drinks in and a bite to eat," I said with a certain degree of contentment that the shift in power was working.

My next stop after leaving the restaurant was plotting up outside Wolfy's house. He was a creature of habit. Saturdays down Millwall, Mondays playing snooker and the remaining days drinking down his local pub the Feathers, which was my next stop as there was little movement in the Wolfy household.

I pushed open the pub door and there was Wolfy chatting to a mate, with a pint in his hand that looked more like a half pint given the size of his mitts. As our eyes met I glanced across to the fireplace and a seated area in the bay window where we could talk. Wolfy concluded his chat, which was no doubt about the Millwall days of the past, when the old Den was a fortress and away teams hated coming to the intimidating ground with its nutty fans. Those were the days.

"Hiya, Wolfy, how are you, mate?"

"Not so bad, Bubs, what brings you down here?"

"I need to have a chat with you. Any more grief from the Old Bill about the Hatton Garden job?"

"No, nothing, they lost interest in me. I think someone must have croaked as they arrested about eight the last I heard," said Wolfy whilst nodding his greetings to a new arrival who was possibly part of Wolfy's Millwall mates, also there to discuss old favourites like Barry Kitchener, Teddy Sheringham and Terry Hurlock.

"Good news. Bet was brilliant at the blag. You would have been proud of her," I said, craning my neck to look him in the eyes.

"Yeah, she said she enjoyed it. Do you want a drink, Bub?"

"No, I'm not staying long, I just needed a quick chat with you. Has Charlie been in touch?"

"No, I thought it was radio silence for two weeks, so I've just kept my head down. I'm surprised to see you here, what's occurring?"

"Wolfy, I know you and Charlie go back a long way and you are one of his best mates, but we have a problem. The value of the job is clear now. Charlie has carved out millions for himself in comparison to what we're due. I'm proposing that all of us involved get equal shares of four million pounds each, and that includes Charlie. I'm not suggesting cutting him out, but twenty million for Charlie compared to our split just isn't right, Wolfy."

"What do you mean you're not cutting him out? He's got the goods or the money by now, so he must be calling the shots," said a frowning Wolfy.

"No, Wolfy, I have the pearls and will keep them until they're sold and I split the money fairly and equally. Pepper and Slippery are both on board and are very disappointed in Charlie trying to shaft us all. So is my brother, Todd, who was our inside man and was offered the same amount as us all – one million – while Charlie pockets twenty times that. We're all together on this new split, Wolfy, and we think you should be in with us too."

As Wolfy was straight lining all the way, I couldn't tell what the hell he was thinking.

"Todd involved?" said monotone Wolfy.

"Yes, he planned the whole thing. Look, I know it's awkward for you. Bet will see the sense in this. She took all the risks and she would want to see a fair split. Talk it through with her. Claudette took the same risk as Bet, so why should she receive twenty times the amount of money you and Bet get. You have plans, Wolfy, and one million won't change your life. But four million... Think about a future with that sort of money. That is only what you and Bet are due."

"Please don't talk to Charlie until you've talked to Bet this evening. You've been loyal to him, but now your loyalty is to Bet and the future. Charlie had planned to rip us all off... All of us. I'll contact you tomorrow, Wolfy. That gives you and Bet time to think."

Wolfy looked bewildered as I left the pub hoping that Bet would come good to guide her husband to the right decision. I drove home to my darling Susie, who thought I had been cabbing all day... Bless her.

CHAPTER THIRTEEN
PEARLS OF WISDOM

I got up early to go to 'work' and threw my sports bag in the cab. When I arrived at the gym, I called Charlie to arrange a time to meet the fence. Charlie hated being forced onto the back foot and not being in control, but he had little choice as at this moment I was holding all the aces. He said the meet had been arranged for eleven thirty at the Waldorf Hotel by the Strand, near theatre land, and I agreed to meet him there.

The hustle and bustle of the area was well known to me. Visitors to London love seeing a show. The experience of *Phantom of the Opera* or *Les Miserables* with a bit of pre-theatre dinner makes for a great night out.

I found Charlie in the lounge area of the hotel. When our eyes met, he had a face like thunder. As I walked towards him, the fence was a few paces behind me, heading, like me, towards Charlie.

Charlie's facial expression changed when he saw the fence. The daggers he had been giving me were replaced by a charming business man. Charlie made the introductions, but no names were exchanged.

"Hello, again. Good to see you." Charlie shock hands with the small, fat man in his mid-fifties, who was wearing a heavy overcoat that was at odds with the weather outside.

Beckoning to me, he said, "This is my colleague. He'll be joining us today in agreeing the way forward."

I shook the fence's hand but he didn't make eye contact. We all sat down and the fence spoke first.

"I need to see the merchandise. We've been discussing it for several months, but I must see the merchandise now." He spat the words out nervously.

I reached in my pocket and took out a cellophane bag containing a dozen pearls, which, after a look over my shoulder, I handed to the fence. His spy glass was raised to his eye and he dexterously inspected the merchandise. He looked up at Charlie.

"Do you have the number of pearls we discussed and are they all of this quality?" he said.

"Yes," said Charlie with a sideways glance at me.

"Then I'll take delivery on Friday and the funds will be in your designated bank account the following working day."

Stretching my hand out to take back the pearls, I returned them to my pocket and responded. "You can take delivery of the pearls on Friday. The funds must be deposited into my designated account on the same day that the merchandise is delivered. I'll advise you of the account details and I need your business card to make contact."

The fence slipped me his card as he began to realise that I was the main player in this game.

"The goods should be delivered to my offices at nine o'clock on Friday morning for inspection before any funds are despatched. The address is on the card. Good day, gentlemen. Until Friday."

Charlie and I stood up to face one another.

"So," said Charlie. "What now?"

"You'll receive four million pounds – the same amount as everyone else."

"I masterminded this job!" Charlie spat the words at me through gritted teeth, poking my chest again with his podgy finger to reinforce his point.

"My dad plotted this blag from the day he put Todd in that company. Without Todd's inside information we would never have pulled this off. And another thing. We were on the job and you weren't – you sent your missus. Why do you deserve twenty million to our one? Answer me that. Claudette deserves the money more than you. Take it or leave it. If you want four million, give me your bank details so I can deposit your funds. If you don't, then go fuck yourself. It's your call."

Charlie pulled out his business card and scribbled the details of his bank account in Gibraltar on the back.

"You don't need to come on Friday, Charlie. I'll deposit your funds the same day. You don't add any value by being there and you don't have the pearls." I was in full swing with Charlie boy now. It's always best to deal with a bully face on.

"You little punk. I'll be there on Friday to make sure this all goes down as I planned. Watch your back, son," Charlie threatened.

"Jog on, Charlie, your day has gone. Watch your back, Sonny Jim – you have many enemies who would love to see you fucked up the arse."

Charlie pushed the revolving doors to leave at the same time as the doorman started spinning them. Jog on was the right expression as he went through the door faster than a Benny Hill sketch, falling on the pavement and throwing a volley of abuse at the unsuspecting doorman... God works in mysterious ways.

I called Todd on his private line and asked him to open a bank account in Bahrain, under Susie's name, where no questions would be asked if high-value deposits were made.

Todd had a good relationship with the bank manager as he often helped wealthy clients to open accounts in Bahrain. He just needed a copy of Susie's passport and a copy of her signature, and he would use his home address as if it were ours.

I suggested he may want me to transfer his share into that account until the heat died down, particularly as Susie still had her maiden name and not ours. He agreed it was a good idea and said he trusted me implicitly.

I told Todd that Susie and I would be travelling to Bahrain on the Monday after the Friday transfer to organise the wedding, so if she needed to go to the bank in person, she could.

I telephoned Pepper and Slippery to arrange a beer down the Blacksmiths Arms that evening, then telephoned Susie to tell her to book flights and hotel for five days in Bahrain to plan our wedding. She was so excited she was about to burst.

I asked if she minded if my mum came so she could play a part with the arrangements and see Todd and Kelly. It would be my treat. Susie got on well with her, so she happily agreed. Mum was thrilled to be invited. She offered to pay her way but I refused.

I was on my way to the Blacksmiths Arms and, boy, was I ready for a good laugh and some banter. It had been quite a week. My mobile rang, and it was Bet. Wolfy had been shot dead in the car park of the Feathers pub. Two shots, both in the face.

Her family were with her, so she said she was okay. Through tears she explained that she knew of the discussion between Wolfy and I. She had an opinion as to who she thought had killed her Wolfy but was keeping it to herself. In the meantime, she told me that both her and Wolfy were totally behind me in what I was doing with the split. I was devastated... Wolfy shot dead!

CHAPTER FOURTEEN
BLACKSMITH ARMS REVISITED

I walked into the Blacksmiths Arms with a heavy heart. The boys were at the bar laughing about something or someone's misfortune.

"Here you go, mate, a pint of Peroni, we saw you pull into the car park," said Slippery. "Pepper's been making me laugh. 'Ere, Bubs, look, they've got a new barmaid. Look at the lungs on her!" He was about to continue when he spotted the grave look on my face. "What's happened, Bubbles?"

"It's Wolfy. Bet called to tell me he'd been found in the Feathers car park. Shot twice in the face... He's dead."

"What the fuck!" Said Pepper.

"Who could have done it?" asked Slippery.

"One guess," I said. "Charlie... It has to be. I met with Wolfy yesterday and told him about the split. He was heading home to discuss it with Bet. I reckon he met up with Charlie and told him he was with us on the four million equal shares. Then Charlie lost the plot and killed him. I can't see it any other way."

"I told you we should have topped him... Now we definitely should," demanded Slippery.

"Let's keep our cool. We're about to become very wealthy. Going to war with Charlie now and bringing the Old Bill sniffing around is not smart. We keep low, support Bet and after the deal's gone through we can get Charlie big bollocks at a later date. The next meet is Friday with the fence. Nine in the morning in Lombard Street, near Bank tube. I'm handing over the pearls in return for twenty-four million pounds, which will be transferred to my bank account. Simultaneously, four million pound transfers will be made to you both, Todd, Bet and Charlie."

"Charlie?" Said Slippery.

"Yes," I said. "It's the same as before the Wolfy business, we have to cut him in or he goes to the Old Bill or tops us like Wolfy. We can sort him out later, but let's put this deal to bed first."

Pepper spoke in a quiet, sad voice. "Firstly, I'm glad that Bet still gets Wolfy's share. I'm not happy about Charlie, but I think you're right about cutting him in. Who's going on Friday to the meet?"

"I am. I said to Charlie that he didn't need to be there, but I don't think I will be able to keep him away. I want both of you there to watch my back, though. We can meet outside the David Lloyd gym at seven fifteen – I'll have the pearls with me. After we get to the fence's address in Lombard Street, wait outside, somewhere you can see the door, and keep half an eye out for any of Charlie's men who may be lurking in the shadows. Don't carry guns, but maybe a persuader in case it kicks off.

"I need you both to open bank accounts soon as and give me the details by Thursday, so I can make the transfers on Friday. Four million pounds hitting the Peckham branch of NatWest may be a little conspicuous so try for a bank account overseas, maybe even a tax haven. Try not to bring attention to yourselves. If you don't feel comfortable then I can leave the money in my overseas account until you have the time to do the research on what is best for you. I'm starting to sound like a wealth management adviser, so I'll shut up."

I paused and softened my voice a little. "I guess we're all a bit shell-shocked with the news about Wolfy, but I hope you have taken in all I've said. We're just a few steps away from getting our money and starting our new wealthier lives. Any questions?"

"Yes. If Charlie has fired a gun, he may be happy to use one again. I think we should be tooled up in case there's a tear up in Lombard Street," said Slippery.

"Fair point," said Pepper.

"It's not in Charlie's interest to top us. He hasn't got his money yet and he won't get any more money if he tops you guys. If he tops me he won't see any money at all. I think the danger comes from him after the split to leverage through fear to get our shares or purely for revenge," I said without any real confidence. After all, we were rationalising about a mad man.

"He may not be stable or logical if he feels he's being shafted," said Pepper.

"But a shoot-out in the city streets full of office workers is not a smart move if you want to remain anonymous. At this moment in time, no one knows who any of us are and that includes Charlie. Listen, Charlie wouldn't want to jeopardise his four million. It's hardly a sum to be sniffed at," I said reassuringly. "I think if he's going to make any sort of move it could be on me, before the meet, to get his hands on the pearls. If we start shooting up the town like cowboys, the fence will go undercover, never to be seen again.

"Let's keep our nerve. It's not too messy at the moment. Get your offshore bank accounts set up. Large sums of money moving around in this country will be reported to the authorities who monitor money laundering so offshore to offshore is best. Be patient and let's get this right without alerting anyone."

'H' brought some drinks over without being asked. He could tell we were in serious discussion. He's a good lad, is 'H'.

"Watch yourselves and I'll see you again on Friday at the gym at seven in the morning. Now let's raise our glasses to an absent friend... To Wolfy."

We stayed a while longer and reminisced about some of the times spent with our much-loved friend. It helped a bit. I drove home and ate some pasta with Susie. I'd eaten so little recently, and with the worrying on top I'd managed to lose half a stone. I told her about Wolfy, the pearls, the blag, the split and Charlie. She cried and cried and cried. I guess I'm not much of a catch as her future husband. She never signed up for all this. I started to worry about her safety in case Susie became a means for Charlie to get to me, so she packed a case and went to stay at my mum's. All a bit short notice but Mum is so streetwise she would be perfect at calming her and putting the best possible perspective on the situation.

I never have had a gun to put under my pillow, but tonight I could have done with one. I locked every door in the house and took a baseball bat to bed with me. That was my sleeping partner that night, not my lovely Susie, and I didn't sleep well. The bat couldn't spoon me the way Susie does.

CHAPTER FIFTEEN
FRIDAY THIRTEENTH

Not the best date in the calendar in terms of luck, but at seven in the morning I was in the gym removing the two cases from locker 333. I placed them in my sports bag along with my sleeping buddy of the previous two nights, the gorgeous baseball bat. We'd become very good friends and recently I hadn't been going anywhere without it.

There was nobody loitering outside the gym and the boys were on time. I didn't ask if they were carrying guns – I didn't want to know. There was no waiting on ceremony and I jumped into the car to get away from there as soon as possible.

We looked like the guy from the Cadbury Milk Tray advert years ago, all of us dressed from head to toe in black... Wallies, who did we think we were? Gangsters!

I suggested we drove to the taxi drivers' café in Shoreditch, leave the car there and hail a cab to take us to the City. It was early morning and it felt autumn like. The trees were starting to turn and the London workers were starting to wear that extra layer of clothing. No one seemed to be following us. We hailed a cab and jumped in, informing the driver of our destination, "Lombard Street, mate." We weren't in the right frame of mind for idle banter, but the cabbie insisted on telling us about the game on TV the previous evening. Costa had been shown the red card and it was his reputation that got him sent off, not the tackle.

The cabbie soon shut up when none of the Milk Tray men responded and we travelled in silence for the rest of the journey. I gave him fifteen quid and told him to keep the change.

We plotted up in a coffee shop across from the fence's office. We could see the entrance to the building and fifty yards up and down Lombard Street, back-dropped by a steady river of people flowing towards their destination. No sign of Charlie or any of his goons – maybe they overslept!

Two espressos later and nine o'clock was approaching. The guys agreed where they were going to stand and left the café first to get into position. I paid for the coffees and exited the café expecting to be shot and left in a pool of blood on the pavement. But no, I made my way across the road and pressed the intercom, stating that I had a meeting at nine, but I did not say who with or who I was. The buzzer spoke back to me and the door pushed open. I looked over my shoulder one last time but there was still no one other than the boys in their positions, looking a bit menacing and surveying the street.

The fence met me in reception and led me to his office. "Would you care for tea or coffee? Is your colleague on his way?"

"No, thanks, no drinks for me. He should be here by now, although he's not required for us to conduct our business."

"Do you have the merchandise with you?" he asked. I passed the cases to him. I'd set them to the right codes so that they could be opened quickly, and he took the samples out and inserted his eye glass to inspect the pearls.

Ten minutes had passed and no sign of Charlie or a shoot-out. I couldn't work it out.

"These are fantastic specimens, as I expected, but nevertheless wonderful to see. I have a buyer in Macau for most of these so they won't be in this country for long. Your colleague doesn't seem interested enough to attend our meeting. His loss and your gain, my friend. The figure agreed is twenty-four million, correct?" said the fat frog from behind his lily pad desk.

"Yes, and here's the bank account in Bahrain where the money should be sent to." I passed him a handwritten note detailing Susie's new bank account.

He lifted the lid of his laptop, keyed in the details and his unique password, pressed send and showed me the payment marked sent.

I called Todd from my mobile to check that the funds had arrived. We then spent a very sweaty five minutes in complete silence waiting for Todd to call back from his secure line. My mobile rang and I could hear Todd's voice at the other end. "The bank manager has confirmed that a very substantial sum of money had been deposited within the last five minutes to the designated account, but it was against the bank's rules to disclose the exact amount other than to the account holder."

"That's good enough for me. Fantastic, speak later," refraining from jumping into the air and performing multiple fist pumps. We both stood up. I gave him the codes to the cases, thanked him for our brief but memorable encounter and left the building.

The boys moved forward as they saw me. We locked eyes and at the same time they both said, "Well?"

"Twenty-four million pounds deposited in my bank ten minutes ago. No sign of Charlie, which is weird but good. Let's get away from here and have a drink."

We marched in the direction of the Lloyds of London building and fell into Balls Brothers wine bar, where we ordered some champagne from a smiling waiter, who said, "Good job guys. Nine forty-five and straight in there with the bubbly. The trading floor must be lively this morning."

"It was a successful piece of business, my good man. How right you are," I said in my plummiest voice and we all cracked up like school children.

We downed three bottles of Veuve Clicquot in an hour and were the noisiest, and only, customers until we walked out into the bright sunlight. How I love London, and never more than on this day.

I had set up automatic payments to go to Pepper and Slippery's offshore accounts and four million pounds to go to Charlie's offshore account in Gibraltar. I was planning on settling up with my brother when we arrived in Bahrain on Monday. Lastly, I would go to see Bet and set up the transfer for her. We hailed a cab and pondered over why Charlie was a no-show. What surprises lay in wait for me now that he had his four million?

We were in with another chatty cabbie. "Did you hear the news this morning? A geezer got shot dead walking down the street. The gunman was riding a motorbike and dressed in leathers. All black and you couldn't see his face. It happened just where I am dropping you off. It's all going mad – shootings in pub car parks and in Shoreditch. It's like living in the States."

We all looked at each other. Without speaking, we knew that it wasn't a bloke on the motorbike. That was our Bet in her leathers, killing the man who had killed her beloved Wolfy. That was why Charlie hadn't turned up... Charlie was dead!

CHAPTER SIXTEEN
THE WEDDING ARRANGEMENTS

I settled with Claudette by telling her to check Charlie's bank account in Gibraltar in case it was a Moody account that he had never told her about. I also suggested she moved the money out of the account *tout suite*, as once she told them he was dead, probate may stop her getting her hands on it for years.

We left for Bahrain with Mum in tow and the five days were fantastic. I had a call from the jewellers. The rings were ready and also a pearl necklace I'd had made for Mum because I'd forgotten to put the original samples back in the briefcase. Silly boy that I am...

No sign of the Old Bill knocking on our or any of the gang's doors, so life was pretty good. No, it was better than that. It was quite unbelievable.

In no time at all we were back at the airport, me, Susie and Mum flying off to Bahrain for the wedding. Todd met us at the other end and told us that he had been interrogated in Bahrain by the Serious Crime Squad from London. He had kept his cool but felt there was a shift in suspicion from the office manager to himself. He even felt that Theo Aqwad was starting to treat him differently. We were all concerned but suggested he stayed calm. It would be difficult to prove any connection between him and the 'gang' as they had no clue who the gang were.

We checked in at the hotel and agreed we'd like to have a nap after the trip, shower then meet up with Todd and Kelly for dinner at eight in the hotel restaurant. Mum asked Todd to invite Theo along, which he agreed to do since Mum had known Theo since the early days. Todd was hesitant – he knew he would feel awkward if he was there at dinner – but Mum was insistent and the invitation was sent. As Todd had mentioned as soon as we arrived, he'd been under the spotlight with the police. I knew he was worried.

Susie went straight to sleep once we were settled in the room, but I was restless. This was the only possible toehold the police had, so Todd had to stay strong under questioning. After an hour, Susie stirred and we showered and changed for pre-dinner drinks. Looking out from the balcony, the sun was setting on an idyllic scene, with the palm trees gently swaying in the evening breeze against a backdrop of the deep blue sky and the Persian Gulf.

Susie can take a while to get ready and I was gasping for a drink so I took myself off to the bar and told Susie I would be back for her in half an hour. Much to my surprise, Mum was already having cocktails with Theo on the veranda. They hadn't seen me come in and I didn't want to be in his company in case he questioned me and I contradicted anything that Todd may have said to him or the police. Mum wasn't wearing her pearl necklace, thank God. She was leaning forward slightly, engrossed in the conversation and looking very elegant. From their body language you could tell they were comfortable with each other, as old friends are.

I demolished two pints of ice cold Peroni and a small plate of nibbles. Feeling hungry, I charged the drinks to my room and gingerly made my way to the lift, avoiding being seen.

Sitting at the dressing table, Susie was drying her hair wearing a white bra and skimpy knickers. She looked drop-dead sexy.

"Hello, gorgeous," I said.

I walked across and kissed her neck then gently massaged her shoulders. I opened my mouth to speak but she beat me to it. "Steady there, tiger, I've showered and am five minutes away from being ready. No time for anything else. Later."

Mmm, I was already aroused. I'm easily excited. "Okay, later." I kissed her neck again and retreated.

The evening meal was very pleasant. Theo was charming. He asked about the wedding and flattered my mum, who loved every minute of it. He didn't mention once that someone had stolen forty million pounds' worth of his pearls, which was odd, but fine by me.

Todd looked washed out and I could tell he was feeling the pressure. Kelly had lost weight in the last month too and both of them looked jaded.

Then Theo looked straight at me and asked, "Did the pearl robbery get much coverage in the UK? Are the police any closer to finding out who robbed me?"

The directness of the question unsettled me at first. "Yes, in the press and on TV. There was another robbery in Hatton Garden, which may have stolen some of the headlines. As for the police getting any closer to finding the thieves, I really wouldn't know. But there's been no reports of people being taken in for questioning." Shut up, Bubbles, I thought to myself. I didn't want this to be the main topic of discussion.

"We've had representatives from Scotland Yard here this week, but I'm not sure what they are expecting to find. Or if they have a plan to arrest anyone."

Mum was the first to speak, "All very distressing for you Theo, but come on. No doom and gloom please. This couple are here to finalise their plans for a wonderful wedding, in your country, Theo."

"I'm so sorry, Daisy," said Theo with great sincerity. Clever old Mum.

"Come on, Theo. Why don't we have a coffee and liqueur at that table looking out to sea and leave the kids to chat." They promptly got up and left.

There was a cloud hanging over us as we sensed there were a few more moves left before this game was over. Not only were we concerned about the police from the UK being here, was Theo suspicious of Todd and the contacts he may have in London's underworld? He must know that our dad was no angel – were we considered to be chips off the old block?

We had a meeting booked with the wedding coordinator at nine thirty the following morning, so we weren't looking for a late night. We ordered coffees and Amaretto liqueurs for the table, had a final chat then said our goodnights to Todd, Kelly, Mum and Theo and made our way back to our room. Susie climbed into bed and registered her concerns for Todd and, ultimately, ourselves. I, too, was worried, but Todd had to remain strong and see them off. The police had nothing on him or any of us, Theo would eventually get his insurance money and we can all move on.

I got into bed and spooned my body next to Susie. Immediately aroused by the warmth of her bottom pressed up against me, I put my arm around her and cupped her breast, and she responded by pushing her bottom hard against me. I turned her to face the pillow and penetrated her from behind as she arched her back to invite me in. I never tire of making love to her. It's rarely just a fuck, but lovemaking with passion and tenderness.

We met Mum for lunch the next day and Susie brought her up to speed on the morning's wedding plans. We were seeing the florist in the afternoon and Mum had arranged to go out with Theo on his boat. Mum had a real glint in her eye and it was so nice to see her enjoying herself. She must have been a stunner in her youth as the years seemed to be dropping off her face since we arrived. She looked twenty years younger. Was this the consequence of a bit of Theo's flattery?

CHAPTER SEVENTEEN
IN THE CELLS

By the evening, the news had broken that Todd had been taken to the police cells for questioning. I jumped in a taxi and made my way to the station to see my brother. It turned out to be a frustrating waste of three hours. They wouldn't let me see him and effectively ignored me.

This was a foreign country and I had no idea how the procedures worked. Did a lawyer need to be present? Did you have the right to remain silent and how long could they hold you in custody without charging you? We needed the help and input of Theo, but he may have been the one to put Todd in the frame. We were forced to leave Todd in the cells overnight and all met for breakfast the next morning to discuss the situation. Kelly looked like she hadn't slept for a week. Thin and gaunt, she cried with worry. She said she felt helpless and didn't know what to do. The same went for all of us, but it was Mum who took the lead.

"You two, Bubbles and Susie, you go about the business you're here for. You need to finalise your wedding plans. Kelly, I know you're worried and, as Todd's mother, I share that worry. But, if Susie doesn't mind, I suggest you spend the day with them helping with their arrangements. It will be good for you to have the company and it will take your mind off Todd. I have Theo's number, so I'll call him and ask for his help."

"Supposing Theo thinks Todd is the inside man though? Why would he want to help? He wants the culprits behind bars," I exclaimed.

"You leave Theo to me. Please go about your business and we can meet for dinner at the hotel this evening. I'll update you on how things are progressing and if I've seen Todd. Kelly, book yourself into the hotel so that you're around family. We are *all* family, so we stick together like glue."

With that, Mum was up and calling Theo on the reception phone. What a leader. Mum was straight in there as head of the family.

Theo picked Mum up from the hotel an hour later. Unaware that Todd had been taken in for questioning, he took Mum straight to his lawyer, briefed him then went directly to the police station. For the time being, Todd was going nowhere, and no amount of pressure could influence our Serious Crime Squad boys.

Theo suggested that he and Mum have a light lunch and a chat. He took her to one of his favourite restaurants, where the tables were perched close to the sea and the water was so close it almost lapped over your feet. After ordering two salads, some locally caught fish and a large bottle of sparkling water, Theo took the stage.

"Before we talk about Todd, I want to say, Daisy, that it has been wonderful to see you and be with you looking so beautiful. When you came to Bahrain a few weeks ago and we met after all this time, you ignited the passion that has been dormant in my heart since we were together briefly all those years ago. I've never married as I never felt the right person had come into my life. You, Daisy, you were the one that had stolen my heart. But, and here is the big but, regardless of my feelings for you, I believe Todd was the voice to the thieves in London who stole my pearls. Originally, I thought it was my office manager as I believe he has been stealing small amounts from me over the years. However, he doesn't have the contacts in London who could pull this off, and he doesn't have the brain power to coordinate it."

Daisy looked intently into Theo's dark and sexy eyes. "What do the police think and have you shared your thoughts with them?" she said unwavering.

"The police have told me, off the record, that they have no suspects as to the gang members in London. Jalal, my office manager, is their main suspect, but they are having difficulty proving his involvement. They think Todd is capable and may have contacts in London. But he has worked honestly and diligently for me for many years and this is totally out of character. He has had many chances in the five years he has been working here, but he has never shown any sign of dishonesty. I guess in the environment of the prison cells, he may feel the pressure and expose himself."

"I don't think you mean expose himself, but I get the drift," mocked Daisy.

"I have no proof, my darling, but knowing Todd's father, Jack, was a villain. Maybe the fruit doesn't fall too far from the bush."

It was getting a little 'Allo! 'Allo! what with Theo's English, but Daisy loved it really.

"You're a silly old sod, Theo Aqwad," said Daisy with a warm smile on her face. "Firstly, thank you for the lovely things you said to me a little while ago. Theo, you have made me feel young and alive again. It has been twenty-nine years since you and I had our affair in London. We were both young, infatuated with each other and a little in love. but I had been married for three years and was still a young girl. I felt that what we were doing was wrong. Jack never ever knew about us. Nobody did. Now you have ignited my passion and, as you say, I have ignited yours. You are a good man, Theo, a lovely man, and there is something you need to know. You say that your suspicions of Todd, who has never stolen from you in five years, is based on the fact that his father was a villain and the fruit does not fall far from the tree, not the bush, Theo, but anyway. Meaning that maybe it follows that Todd must be a villain too? Theo, you are Todd's father... Yes, you! Have you never looked at his eyes, those beautiful dark eyes, and not seen yourself? I could never tell you, Jack or Todd."

Daisy waited for Theo's reaction. People use the word dumbstruck, and Daisy was looking at a man who was totally lost for words. Daisy sipped her water and smiled. Theo eventually spoke gently and slowly. Every word was tinged with love.

"Our son, Todd... Our son. I've loved him as if he were my own these last five years without ever realising he is my, *our* son! Oh, Daisy, I love you more than ever, what a day. Waiter! Champagne please. We have to celebrate, Daisy, my love."

"A minor celebration, Theo, as our son is still in custody," said a glowing Daisy.

"Oh, yes, yes, I agree," stuttered Theo.

They raised their glasses to toast 'our son Todd'. Theo downed the drink in one as Daisy sipped hers.

"Another toast to us and our future together!" said Theo, wide-eyed and hopeful.

"One ground-breaking piece of news in a day is quite enough I think," said Daisy with compassion. "But I do think you, me and Todd should be seeing much more of each other. Now, come over here and give me a kiss."

Theo leapt to his feet, kissed the love of his life and proceeded to do a sort of Irish jig as he danced round the table in sheer joy.

Todd was released from prison as there was insufficient evidence to convict or hold him in the cells any longer. The Serious Crime Squad returned to London the same day.

CHAPTER EIGHTEEN
LOVE EVER AFTER

The Indian office manager Jalal resigned, with a little encouragement from Todd, and returned to his homeland. Todd was told about his new father, which didn't come as a massive surprise to Todd, who knew only too well how his eyes were his main pulling tool with the girls before Kelly was on the scene, and they were identical to Theo's eyes.

The wedding was brilliant, and Susie and I could not have been happier. Our first baby is due any time now. We're looking for a bigger home in Blackheath and a clothes shop for Susie. Mum is radiant and Theo and her are like teenagers in love. Mum is in Bahrain more than she is in London and looking like a thirty-year-old. Todd has been made a partner in Theo's business and dates for their wedding are in place for the autumn. The plan is to make their permanent home in Bahrain, but I still think he misses London.

Pepper, Slippery, Janice and Julie have pooled their money and bought a mansion in La Zagaleta in Marbella. Drinking, eating, boats, water skiing and golf. Pretty much living the good life, just spending their money.

Claudette has been busy with cosmetic surgery. She looks amazing, weighs next to nothing and has a new boyfriend who is nineteen years of age! Go for it, girl...

Bet has found it hard without Wolfy, but she's joined various bikers' clubs and is often crossing continents on her Harley wearing her infamous black leathers.

So, we're all happy, healthy, wealthy and wise enough to be keeping out of trouble. I will leave it a few years and may just summon the team for a modest quencher at the Blacksmiths Arms for old times' sake and see if anyone is bored and looking for a bit of excitement!

PART TWO

CHAPTER ONE
FIVE YEARS LATER

I fill my days playing a bit of golf, in the gym, the occasional weekend away with the gun club shooting game, or with the kids. It wasn't how I imagined being very wealthy would be, to be honest. As the old saying goes, be careful what you wish for. Money was always a motivator for me, but I was finding out that the chase is better than the kill. I don't go down the Blacksmiths Arms much as all my mates have moved on to greener pastures. It's the banter I miss most of all and the piss-taking. I don't even have anyone to moan to about Millwall football team.

Being married is everything I hoped it would be, and the kids are a dream. We have two little tadpoles, Oliver who is four and little Daisy who's one. Both blond and beautiful. We now live in a lump of a gated house in Blackheath, which was built in the Edwardian period. With its high ceilings, huge rooms with sash windows and six bedrooms, it's a truly fabulous home in a great location.

We never had any repercussions from the police, either in Bahrain or London. Theo hasn't mentioned the robbery to Todd since the wedding, so everything is sweet there.

Susie and I have made close friends with Michael and Francesca, who live a few streets away from us in

Blackheath. Susie met Francesca at the anti-natal clinic when Oliver was on his way into the world. I took to Michael the first time I met him. It was in our local Italian and three blokes at another table were pissed, swearing and generally getting on everyone's nerves, shouting their mouths off. Francesca is particularly attractive, well, stunning in fact, and these guys had clocked her and one of them was saying something very inappropriate, which Michael and the whole restaurant heard. Michael stood up and slowly walked to their table. Luigi, the restaurant owner, saw the situation brewing and started to make his way there. Susie had been telling me earlier in the evening what a lovely couple they were and that their son was the same age as Oliver and are best mates at nursery school.

I decided that the odds were a bit stacked in the rowdy guys' favour if it kicked off, so I got up and stood alongside Michael for support.

Michael said, "It's been an entertaining evening for everyone in the restaurant listening to your words of wisdom. Particularly you, my friend, who was so descriptive of my wife's body."

"But like all good things, they must come to an end. Boys, it's time for you to go. Luigi, their coats please.'"

The loudmouth went to stand up, but as he pushed his chair back it caught in the carpet and he was left in an awkward squatting position, trying to look tough. Michael continued in the same even tone.

"Don't even think about it, son. Do yourselves a favour and call it a day. Don't come round my manor again, now jog on before this all turns very nasty." Michael threw two hundred pounds onto the table and said, "For the inconvenience to your diners, Luigi."

They all stood up, I guess they never had any coats, because under Michael's steady glare, they exited the restaurant without any contribution to the cost of their meal or to any further conversation. It was a masterful demonstration on how to deal with a tricky situation from Michael, without violence, swearing or once raising his voice. Just his presence, and choice of words that carried a slightly threatening overtone.

To finish this masterclass of style, he came over to thank me for standing shoulder to shoulder with him and offered to buy us a drink. We have been close friends, the four of us, from that night on. He's a star.

Needless to say I don't drive the black cab anymore and keep myself to myself, which leads to a fairly lonely existence. I try not to get involved in small talk with people I meet. I guess Michael is the only one I chat with, but never about the past events or how I have so much money. Although Michael and Francesca live local, their house is modest compared to ours. Michael works for De Beers as a buyer and often travels to South Africa with the job. Francesca is a full-time mother and housewife and was previously a hairdresser. They were both born locally and were childhood sweethearts, but after a few years apart they reconnected and have been together ever since.

Michael went to a good grammar school and is a bright, streetwise guy – a great combination. He is a trader and I suspect he could sell razorblades to the Taliban if he put his mind to it. Francesca cuts Susie's hair and colours it. I often wonder how Susie deals with any awkward questions about us, particularly as the pair of them don't stop talking when they're together.

It was a bitter cold Wednesday morning, ten o'clock, the time I take our dog, Bull's Eye, an English Bulldog, for a walk. I go to the Heath and let him have a run off the lead. It's very quiet at that time, and although the dog isn't violent, he hates other dogs and will see them off.

I was lobbing a tennis ball and Bull's Eye was chasing and returning the ball to me when I spotted two guys walking towards me. A little unusual to see anyone other than dog walkers at that time of day midweek, and who would want to be going for a stroll in these arctic conditions. They had a purposeful stride, but where were they going? There was only me in the direction they were travelling.

As they approached I could see they were about twenty-five years of age and looked very similar, like brothers. They were heading for me all right. I kept the dog, who had his tongue flopped out of the side of his mouth panting after his exercise, by my side.

"Hello, Bubbles, how are you," said one of the young guys.

"How do you know me?" I said holding his stare.

"You don't remember us, do you?"

"No, I don't," I replied.

"We're Charlie's twin boys. I'm Charles and this is John. I think we need to have a little chat about the good old days, Bubbles, when you never had a pot to piss in and our dad was alive."

Fuck… This was out of the blue. I'd forgotten about them. They had been farmed off to board at fee-paying schools since they were about five.

"How can I help you, boys. This seems as good a place as any to chat," I said, still keeping strong eye contact.

"You owe us some money. We feel that you know the details of our dad's death. You owe us, Mr Fucking Bubbles," said Charles, who had done all the talking so far.

"The first thing for you to do Mr Tweedledee and Mrs Fucking Tweedledum is go talk to your mother, she can tell you all you want to know," I said with a snarl. "Don't turn up on my doorstep with your public school silly voice trying to put the squeeze on me because it won't wash. Now, go and talk to your mother before I set the dog on you pair of Nancy boys."

"We want five million pounds. We don't care how you get it, just get it. We shall talk again soon and you better have a good plan for getting the money because our plummy voices will be well heard and understood by Scotland Yard when we tell them what we know. Don't underestimate us. We'll give you a week, so be here the same time next Tuesday."

With that they turned on their polished Churches shoes and left the Heath.

CHAPTER TWO
THE EIGHT CLUB

I went home to think. This pair of shits were not going away and I needed a plan. I had to speak with the boys, my boys, as this could affect us all. I had to get word to meet up at the Blacksmiths Arms for a tête-à-tête. I needed to nip this in the bud before the twins got too trappy.

But first I needed to speak with the twins' mum, Claudette. I had an old mobile number for her but had no idea if it was still in use. It rang twice and she picked up.

"Hi, Claudette, it's Bubbles, how are you," I asked, half guessing her reply

"The gorgeous Bubbles calling little ole' me. Have you dumped that silly bit of stuff you used to knock around with and are calling for me to satisfy all your sexual fantasies?"

"That's my wife and mother of my children you are referring to, you naughty girl," I said with a smile.

"I can show you how naughty I can be if you let me!"

I didn't answer her but continued. "I need to see you on a serious matter, Claudette. When are you free to meet?"

"Now, my boyfriend's the jealous type and he's not back home until later this evening. So not near here. What about my club in the City? It's full of business types, and I can book a small office for privacy.

"It's the Eight Club EC3, near Bank tube. See you there in two hours. You can buy me lunch. Bye." And she was gone.

I got changed, took a taxi and was at the Eight Club in Change Ally within two hours. I pressed the intercom and the door sprung open. It was like an old bank vault. I descended the spiral staircase to reception, where I signed in as a guest of Claudette. She hadn't arrived yet, so I ordered a drink and took in my surroundings.

It reminded me of an American speakeasy from the prohibition days. Not really where I would have placed Claudette, but maybe that was why she liked it. It was her club and full of men from the City. I bet her child boyfriend didn't know about this place.

Claudette arrived. Wow, the whole place went quiet as she glided across to my table with a fur coat on that probably cost more than Millwall's midfield. She looked expensive, glamorous and had every table wondering how old she was. She looked good, but... Still not for me.

"Hi, Claudette. You look fabulous and younger than ever," I said. Well, it was half right.

"Oh, Bubbles, you are so fuckable," said Claudette, crossing her legs as the fur fell away and revealed her slim legs. Now the whole club was thinking 'has she got anything on under that fur coat?' My guess was a thong and little else.

"Some bubbly, Claudette?"

"What else, my darling? They know what I like. It'll be here in a mo."

I was just a 'blow on' in this theatrical extravaganza. There was only one performer worth watching.

We took our drinks to the office and ordered a light lunch.

"What is troubling you, Bubbles?" said Claudette after her first sip of champagne slid down her unwrinkled neck.

"Your twin boys, Claudette. They're putting the squeeze on me for five million pounds or they said they'd blab to the Old Bill about the past. Do you know anything about this?"

"Nothing," said Claudette with the same look on her face as the time we were travelling to the blag and the penny dropped as to how dangerous it was. "I haven't seen those boys in years. They stayed at Charlie's mum's during the school holidays and when they left school, or in reality were expelled, they moved into a flat together near Marylebone, I think. They haven't spoken to me since Charlie's funeral. They somehow held me responsible for his death.

"They are wrong 'uns, Bubbles, be careful. I know I was never much of a mother to those boys, but they're violent, and the way they look at me makes my blood curdle."

"But if they shop us it implicates you. Don't they see that?" I pointed out.

"I don't think it would bother them. If they could lay the blame for Charlie's murder at my door, they would."

"It doesn't sound as if they would listen to you if you tried to talk them round. What about Charlie's mum, their nan. Would they listen to her?"

"No. They idolise their nan because she brought them up really. But she lets them do what they want as she thinks that guarantees their love for her. All their aggression comes from that side of the family."

There was a knock on the door and our waitress entered carrying a tray with two plates of prawns, crab meat and a small salad with brown sesame rolls. I will need some pie and mash when I leave because these are children's portions. No wonder Claudette has a great figure.

The waitress left, closing the door behind her.

"Not good, Claudette. Any suggestions on how to call your boys off before they blab?"

"None at the moment, but I'll think about it and let you know," she said. It was the longest and most sensible conversation I'd ever had with Claudette, and although it was bad news, I thought how sweet she could be. It was short-lived.

"Do you know why I like these offices so much, Bubbles? Let me tell you. They have no cameras."

With that she stood up, slipped off her fur coat and let it fall to the floor. I was wrong with my guess as to what she had on under the fur because it was nothing. She was completely naked.

She had now taken on a Russian voice and was sliding across the table towards me. "Vould sir like me to suck his Vlodivostok?" she said as her face arrived facing my crotch.

"No, sir would not, my Russian beauty. Sir would like to get the bill and work out how to deal with my Russian princess's bastard kids. Come on, put your fur on and let's get you home to Siberia." It would be so easy to cave in to Claudette, but I just couldn't do it.

We left the club and I stuck the disappointed Claudette into a cab, although it was all theatre to her.

I had to pull the guys together, as well as Bet, so I started contacting them that afternoon. I suggested a Monday lunchtime meet at the Blacksmiths Arms. Todd was back in the UK on a business trip without Kelly, so the timing was perfect. Pepper and Slippery were easy to contact. They were just a couple of hours away in Spain and agreed to be there. Bet was a little harder to track down as she was in Jersey, but her bike race was on the Saturday, so Monday was fine with her.

I didn't have a solution in my mind, but maybe an alcohol-fuelled brainstorming session may provide an answer. Although when it came to us being a think tank, we were more tank than think.

Susie had taken the kids to Francesca's for some food and for the girls to have a little Prosecco and a lot of chat. I suggested that Michael and I popped down the local as I was ready for couple of pints with a mate.

We went to the Nag's Head. They do a variety of real ales, which are not really for me as I'm lager drinker, but I knew Michael liked them. Michael wasn't into football, so no banter there. I think he's the only friend I have who doesn't even like to talk about football, even if he never plays.

We strode out together from his house. It was freezing outside and not a night for a leisurely stroll. The pub had a warm, welcoming orange glow, and the path was clear to get my belly up to the bar and order a Peroni. I knew it would take Michael longer to peruse the blackboard listing all the guest beers and their strengths before deciding.

"A pint of Black Dog," he said thoughtfully, which was a mild bitter. I had never drunk mild, but as it was poured it looked like a dark Guinness. Not such an intense black, more a dark nutty brown colour. It looked great, to be honest.

"Cheers," I said. "Did you have a good day?"

"Yeah, not bad. Most days are the same for me, but once in a while an expensive diamond hits the market that causes the traders to get excited. The history of some of the better-known diamonds is really interesting."

"My great-great nan was in service as a cook to one of the richest diamond families in the world. The stories were passed down at Sunday teatime as we ate cockles and winkles with bread and butter."

"That's cool. What's the story there then?"

"It was a family called the Joels out of the East End. Solly Joel worked down Petticoat Lane and also did a bit of variety on the stage with his cousin, a bloke called Bernato. Long story short, they both ended up in South Africa prospecting for diamonds and came good."

"In 1905 they, or their miner named Robert Powell, discovered the Cullinan Diamond or the Great Star of Africa, which was the largest diamond in the world weighing in, rough and unpolished, at three thousand-plus carats. It was cut into nine major stones and ninety-six smaller ones. The Cullinan I and Cullinan II are set in the Sceptre and the Imperial State Crown, both of which are part of the Crown Jewels. Sorry to be such a nerd with this stuff. I don't mean to bore you."

"Not at all, it's fascinating. So, what happened to the two East End chancers?" I asked.

"The cousin met with an untimely end. He went overboard on a ship while having a stroll along the decks with Solly Joel. His death was unsolved and may have been suicide. Solly was left with the fortune."

Solly then became chairman of De Beers. They were his main competitor in the diamond mines of South Africa. He was one of the richest men in the world. Solly had three children, one of whom was Stanhope Joel, racehorse owner and entrepreneur. My great-great grandmother was the cook at their family home in Mayfair."

"What a story," I said in awe. It certainly was a different type of conversation to the normal banter with my mates down the Blacksmiths Arms.

Michael ordered another round of drinks. "So, do you have a high-powered position at De Beers and do they know this story?" I asked.

"No. They're a toffee-nosed lot and if I was to say my family were in service to the Joels they would take the piss, so I've never mentioned it. And no, I'm not a top earner there and promotion is a lengthy process if it ever comes your way. In fact, Francesca and I are thinking of moving to South Africa to see if there are better opportunities out there. I have some good friends at our offices in Johannesburg and the cost of living may give us a better quality of life."

"Oh, I would hate for you to emigrate! I don't have many friends that I can call good friends, but you're right up there, Michael. Can I help in any way?"

"No, mate, I don't think so. Anyway, I don't know anything about you and Susie. You have a fantastic house but I have no idea what you do for a living, Bubs," enquired Michael.

I had rehearsed my stock response, which Susie had been briefed on so as to be consistent. I was confident that Susie would have given the same story to Francesca.

"Well, Michael, I don't work too much these days. I had a bit of luck on the lottery, which really set us up, and I keep my head above water betting online on the horses, football, cricket. Basically, anything I can make a profit on."

"Can I ask how much you won?"

"Yeah, a million plus. We have been really lucky," I replied. I hated lying to him and wanted to tell him the truth, but that wasn't possible. I moved the subject on to a couple of girls in the pub who had been looking over at us on and off since we walked in.

"Have you clocked the two blondes giving us the evil?" I said, moving my head in their direction.

"Yes, I know one of them from a club I used to go to before Francesca, I just can't remember her name," said Michael.

"I think they know we're talking about them. They're on their way over."

"Hello, Michael, long time no see. This is my friend Patsy and I am Janice, if you don't remember," she said with a smile.

"Of course I remember! Janice, how are you? What's new? Oh, sorry, this is my mate Bubbles."

"Hi, Bubbles," said Patsy. They had already worked out who was having who, as Janice sidled up to Michael.

"What's new with you girls?" I said to Patsy, repeating the question.

"Well, we're not married and we are looking for Mr Corporate to take us away from all this. Could that be you two? Or are you like most of the guys we meet – full of shit and pushing dope?"

"No," I said. "Not on a Wednesday. Wednesdays we are invincible, Thursdays we help the aged and Fridays we walk the kids to school. Not what you are used to, but I don't think we are for you either."

"Your mate's quick through the gate. You got kids, Michael?" Janice asked.

"Yes. Did you ever marry Johnny Rolfe from Peckham?" asked Michael as he began to place where he knew Janice from.

"Yes, and what a wrong 'un he turned out to be. He's doing a ten-year stretch in Belmarsh nick for drug smuggling. That's where your dad is, ain't he, Mike?"

Michael shot a glance at me. That piece of information had slipped under the radar, not that it bothered me.

Michael didn't answer and just gave a look that let Janice know she'd said too much.

Patsy chipped in. "Well, if you two ain't gonna buy us a drink we're offski. As they say in Russia, Moscow."

With that they were gone and we both had a good laugh.

I didn't ask any more questions about his dad and left it for Michael to say something if he wanted to.

We got back to Francesca and Susie and made tracks for home immediately as the kids were tired.

The next morning I was walking Bull's Eye, as always, when a black van raced across the Heath heading in my direction. I called Bull's Eye over as the van stopped and the doors flew open. Three guys got out carrying baseball bats and wearing dark clothes and balaclavas. There was nowhere to hide and running seemed pointless as they circled me. The first strike I didn't see coming and it rocked the back of my head and dropped me to the floor. Groggy, I got back on to my feet. Staying down was a guarantee for a beating.

I threw a punch that disappeared into the air without landing and then the blows just rained down on my head, back, legs and anywhere else that was exposed. I was an easy target. Bull's Eye was going nuts, growling and snapping, then it all went black.

I awoke in a hospital bed in A&E with a doctor and nurse standing over me. "How are you, sir," said the doctor. "We're very pleased to see you awake, you took quite a beating."

"Where's the dog?" I asked.

"I'm very sorry to say that your dog is dead. Your wife is in the waiting room. Would you like to see her? The police would like a word, but we can keep them at bay until you're ready," he said in a caring voice.

"Yes, wife." I could just about get the words out as my mouth and nose felt like they were full of blood and snot.

Susie came through the gap in the curtain surrounding my bed. Her eyes were full of tears and she stroked my hair with all the softness she could manage with her shaking hand.

"The dog's dead. I'm sorry," I spluttered.

"I know, but you're not, my sweet. We've all been so worried. Who did this to you?"

"I don't know. What's the damage?" I asked.

"Broken nose, cheekbone, hand, three broken ribs and multiple bruises, lacerations and probably concussion. Otherwise, you're perfect," she said with tears in her eyes.

"Two dog walkers found you left for dead. I just cannot believe this happened to you."

"If they wanted me dead, I'd be dead," I whispered. Tired and full of morphine, I couldn't keep my eyes open and drifted off to sleep.

CHAPTER THREE
BACK TO THE BLACKSMITHS ARMS

I woke and had some soup and bread, which tasted fabulous. Soon after, the police interviewed me for descriptions of the attackers and if it was retaliatory in any way. I told them I didn't know them and there were no vendettas that I knew about. They left empty handed and I discharged myself and got a taxi home.

Susie went mad at me and said I should be back in hospital recuperating. I kissed her forehead, said nothing and headed for my armchair that looked out toward the gardens. I knew who did it. If not them personally, then their cronies. Mum telephoned from Bahrain and Todd called from his hotel, both enquiring how I was. But I didn't want them to visit and I made light of it all.

I had a few days to get myself together before the meet on Monday with the guys. I was still going without a Plan A, B or C, hoping we would find the best solution between us.

Michael popped in on Sunday evening to see how I was.

"I've seen you look better, Bub. The bruising on your face is coming out and your eyes, nose and cheek are all black." He shook his head. "There are some nasty fuckers around. Susie said you have no idea who did this to you?" He looked at me in the same way he'd looked at me that evening in the restaurant. His face and eyes were almost saying don't take me for a fool, I can sort this out.

"No, mate, I don't know who they were."

There was a long pause before Michael spoke. "Bubbles, I'm your mate. If you need my help, I'm here. I'm not prying into your business, but I don't buy all this 'I won the lottery' and 'I don't know who they were'. If you're in some sort of trouble, you should tell me. I can't help if I don't know the problem."

"I can't tell you, Michael, I just can't. I really appreciate your friendship but there are other people in the mix and their safety is at stake too. When and if the time is right I'll tell you everything, but not now. Please understand and respect my position." I said. "Now, help yourself to a beer in the fridge."

"It's okay, I need to get back. I'll pop in during the week to see how you are. Maybe bring you some dirty mags – they should sort you out. I'll let myself out. Take good care of yourself, Bub."

I couldn't wait until Monday lunchtime when I could offload and share some of this with the gang, as well as seeing my lovely mates again.

'H' greeted me at the door. "Hello, son. What the fuck has hit you – a truck?"

"No, 'H', three trucks carrying baseball bats," I said and winced.

"I need some privacy, 'H', some of the old faces should be here soon. Is the back room free?"

"Sure. It may be a bit cold but I'll open it up and put the heater on," he said.

I had dropped 'H' twenty-five thousand pounds a little while after the blag. He'd had been as good as gold at keeping quiet about our meetings in the pub and the murder in his car park, so I felt he'd earned it. My ribs were still sore, so I perched myself on a stool in the back room as 'H' slid across a pint of Peroni. My mind went back to Charlie using the dartboard's blackboard to crudely chalk the route of the limousine and our vehicle positions for the robbery. I could see Claudette with her crossed legs, sitting on a bar stool reading her magazine or newspaper. It had been five years since then and so much had changed for us all.

The noisy raucous laughter that filled the air told me that Pepper and Slippery were in the house, with Bet following, giggling to herself. Shortly after, Todd arrived, apologising for being late. He'd forgotten how to get to the Blacksmiths Arms. I chose not to invite Claudette as her loins had produced the problems we were about to discuss. Everyone looked so tanned except me. I was looking like shit and felt like the oldest person there.

We all exchanged hugs and kisses, and 'H' was on hand to take the drinks order. We swapped a few stories and updates on our lives, but everyone was really waiting to hear about the problem we had.

"Guys, guys, thanks so much for coming. You don't know how much I've missed you all and our drinking sessions at the Blacksmiths Arms. But we have a potential problem that I'm hoping we can resolve together."

"As you can see, I've taken a bit of a hiding from some thugs and I don't believe it was random. Last week, Charlie's boys, the twins, paid me a visit, threatening to go to the authorities about the blag and Charlie's murder. They want five million to keep quiet, and I have until tomorrow to come up with how I am going to raise the dough. The outcome, if they grass, affects all of us so I thought it best to call this gathering.

"I also met with Claudette to ask if she knew anything about the twins' actions and what they knew. It was evident that they have never been part of her life and she has lost any contact with them. Apart from being away at boarding school, the grandmother had played the role of mother. The boys are living together in a flat in Marylebone."

It took a few minutes for the team to process the information.

"How old are the boys now?" asked Bet.

"I would say mid-twenties."

"Did they do this to you?" asked Todd.

"If not them, then their cronies. There were three of them with baseball bats and their faces were hidden. We've had no comebacks from the police since the robbery, it couldn't have gone better, but if they blab we could all be doing time, and a lot of it."

Todd was the first to propose a solution. "They may be bluffing and know very little. When you meet them, ask some leading questions to uncover how much they know. After all, none of us have spoken to anyone in five years so why have they taken so long to apply the pressure."

"Unless they've only just found out," said Pepper, "which is feasible. But from who?"

"We have enough money between us to put a million pounds in the pot each and pay them off," said Bet, who had the most to lose.

Slippery responded, "But they'll just come back for more. Nothing will have changed. I say top 'em."

That was fairly predictable from Slippery. Bet spoke again.

"Look, I've done it once and I can kill again. I would get life in prison if I was convicted for killing one or three people."

"We could, as Bet said, put a million in each, but with my lifestyle, the money's going fast," said Pepper.

"That goes for me, too," said Slippery. "I would sooner do another job than use the last of my money. Me and Pepper are getting bored anyway, drinking and laying in the sun every fucking day with just the women for company. It's not as if we can pop down the boozer and have a chat like we used to. We have to be so careful who we let into our lives."

Todd returned to his first topic. "They may have some information, from whom I'm not sure, but I think we should play hardball and flush out what they know. We need more info on the twins. Claudette may have seen them, even briefly, and let something slip. We need to find out more about Claudette's boyfriend. What do we know about him?"

"Nothing, other than he's in his twenties," I said.

"Well, let's start making some enquiries about him. Has he got form? Does he know the twins? What do we know about the twins, anything?"

"Expelled from school, violent nature like their dad. That's about all," I said, realising we had more questions than answers. "Okay, I'll stall for time and ask more questions. See if I can buy another week to get more intelligence on the twins and Claudette's boyfriend," I said.

"Do you want us to come with you, Bubs? To show some force," said Pepper.

"No, Pep, if he's bluffing and doesn't know that much about who we are, we don't want him to see faces he could put to the blag. But thanks, mate.

"Okay, actions… I will go to the meet tomorrow on my own and stall for time and try to find out what they really know.

"Todd, you can go to their school. I think it was Dulwich College. Say you are returning to this country and a friend had suggested Dulwich as a great school for the kids. Use Claudette's name and see what reaction and info about the twins you can glean.

"Pepper and Slippery, I'm not sure how, I'll leave that to you, but find out what you can about Claudette's bloke. His name, who he knocks around with, what he does for a living.

"Bet, I can't think of a role for you at the moment, but please stay local and let's all meet again down here Friday lunchtime at twelve o'clock for an update. In the meantime, let's catch up tonight and find out what everyone has been up to."

CHAPTER FOUR
INTELLIGENCE

We finished the evening embracing each other in the car park, pissed and all loved up after spending time together again. Even though it might have been the drink talking, no one seemed ecstatic with their lives and I know they would come back to the old haunts at the drop of a hat. Money had changed us all, but I'm not sure if it was all for the good. Todd came back to mine and in the morning he cancelled his hotel room.

On the Tuesday morning I made my way to the Heath and sat on a bench close to where I'd been attacked. I wasn't feeling sorry for myself but I was thinking about my lovely dog that they had ruthlessly killed. It was a bright start to the day and the dog walkers were scattered around the Heath, which is vast. Their silhouettes against the low sun made them look like the matchstick men in Lowry's paintings.

I could see two figures walking in my direction. Soon the twins would be with me. My initial thoughts were to tear into them and rip them apart but, in reality, with my ribs broken and a busted hand, I was in no condition to fight anyone. It was only the morphine patches and painkillers that hid the pain of my bruised and battered body.

"Bubbles, what have you been up to since we last met, you look as if you've done ten rounds with David Haye," said the cocky Charles, who was the mouthpiece for the twins.

"No, not David Haye, just three cowardly girls pretending to be tough," I replied with a sneer on my battered face.

"So, Mr Bubbles, where are we with our money?" asked Charles.

"I know nothing about your dad's death and I certainly don't have money to give you. Not five million or five quid. I don't know where you're getting your intelligence from but it's not kosher."

"Don't be silly, Mr Bubbles, we know all about the blag, all the money you got and how you arranged the hit on our dad. Pearls wasn't it? Very nice. Well, it's payback time now," said the arrogant Charles.

"Who told you it was me that did that blag? I read the papers just like you and it was about five years ago now and nothing to do with me. Neither was your dad's death. Who is telling you this crap?"

"Never mind who told us. Five million or we go to the police. You and my dad did the blag with a couple of his mates and then you topped him so you could have his share of the loot. My dad is dead now, so they can't prosecute him for the robbery, but they can you."

"Go back to your source and arrange a meet with him and me. It's just someone who has beef with me and wants to finger me for a job I know nothing about. How long have you known your informant, how trustworthy is he?" I said.

The twins looked at each other with a slight grin and John spoke for the first time.

"How long?" John repeated. "All our lives! Is that long enough?"

Charlie shot John a look and told him to shut up, but the cat was out of the bag. It must be Claudette who was blabbing to the boys or pillow talk with her boyfriend. Maybe they didn't know that Claudette was on the team as he said 'a couple of his dad's mates'. As planned, I needed to stall for time and to meet with my guys on Friday to see what info we had gathered.

"I was not a part of this blag. You seriously need to check your source. And as for you two going to the police with this cock and bull story, with your history, it's a joke. If your dad's killer was one of his mates you should watch yourselves because if they've killed once they won't think twice before killing you two if they feel the pressure is on. So, fuck off, don't bother me again and don't go anywhere near my family or I will kill you both myself."

Charlie replied. "You've got one month to come up with the money. We'll be in touch. Not got your dog with you today, Bubbles?"

I was on the verge of flying at him and ripping his throat out, but I knew my body was too fragile and once the adrenaline rush had subsided I would be too weak to fight.

"One day, Charlie boy, one day and you will wish you had never met me."

As they sloped away I heard a noise behind me. Not another beating, I thought, but it was my brother, Todd, dressed like an Antarctic explorer. He had his anorak hood up and a scarf around his face, but his eyes were showing and there was no mistaking my Todd.

"I thought my big brother may need some help," he said. "There's another face over there who I thought might be with the twins. He seemed interested in what was going on, but he's walking away now so I don't think he was with them."

I looked across at the tall figure walking towards the road. It was Michael looking out for me in case I needed help. On the road was a figure on a motorbike dressed in black leathers. It could only be Bet. She powered up the engine and drove off. Todd had all sorts of armoury under his coat, including a truncheon, a carving knife and a sword. As it turned out, I wasn't alone after all.

Todd and I strolled back to my house. I told him about Michael and what a good friend he had become, but that I'd never told him about the robbery. I also said how concerned I was for Susie's safety and that I was planning on asking her to take the kids to Mum's for a while. Todd agreed it was a good idea and he told me he was going to delay returning to Bahrain until things were more settled here.

Susie left with the kids, who loved sleeping over at their gran's house, and Susie's mum loved having them. Todd had an appointment at Dulwich College the next day to find out anything he could about the twins.

I needed to see Claudette to fully understand what she had said and how much the twins knew, and then I needed to get a gun for protection. I had a licence as I'd got into shooting at the gun club, who met every weekend to shoot game. We often went to Scotland in the grouse season. It was one of those things I took up as I had so much time on my hands, but recently I'd lost interest. I hadn't attended any meets or weekends away for a good few months now. The licence was handy. No questions would be asked if I bought a gun.

I telephoned Claudette and asked to meet her the next day. She was a little reluctant but eventually she told me to come to Champneys spa resort in Tring, where she was pampering herself for five days. She suggested I bring my swimwear and I could spend the day there as her guest. Thankfully Susie would not be around to see me going off to spend a day frolicking in the pool with Claudette. More secrets, which I didn't like, but sometimes they are a necessary evil.

I drove through the countryside of the Chiltern Hills to Tring, enjoying the views along the country lanes and admiring the great properties, from thatched-roof houses to huge manor houses with sweeping drives and manicured lawns. Red kites peppered the skies with their vast wings gliding through the air looking down for unsuspecting pray. With their squawking cries penetrating the quiet countryside, they were the closest bird to an eagle I'd ever seen.

I arrived at the impressive grounds of Champneys resort and admired the huge manor house containing the pools, spa, restaurant and accommodation. I went to reception and advised them that I was a day guest of Claudette. Claudette is like Boris Johnson, the ex-Mayor of London. Everyone knows her by her first name, you don't need to use her surname.

They escorted me to where she was having a facial and I pulled up a chair alongside her. She couldn't speak or the mask could crack. The torture women put themselves through in an attempt to remain beautiful and keep the years at bay.

Claudette was wearing a white, waffle-type robe with Champneys embroidered on the chest pocket, with her hair tied back in a ponytail. They removed the mask and moisturised her skin, leaving a face I didn't recognise. Claudette with no makeup, red lipstick or false eyelashes looked older but, I thought, more beautiful. Childlike and vulnerable.

"Hello, Bubbles. Don't stare, I must look awful."

"You look beautiful, Claudette, just beautiful. Don't worry about makeup. Just stay as you are."

"Never," she said. "Come on, let's go in the jacuzzi together. Have you brought your swimming stuff?"

"Yes, I've got my trunks on under my tracksuit."

"So coy, Bubbles."

We walked along the corridor and I could smell the chlorine. The automatic doors opened to the pool. The jacuzzi and rooms for steam and sauna were to the rear of the pool. We both slid into the bath-warm water and Claudette hit the button to start the bubbles. It was a lovely sensation and, true to form, Claudette slipped her bikini bottoms off, threw her head back and arched her body, closing her eyes.

I could feel myself becoming aroused. What did I expect? I should have known that she would be like this. Her hand reached across and held my penis. I could feel myself going hard in her grip. She released her hold and, with both hands, pulled my trunks down. We looked at each other for a second and then she submerged herself under the water after saying "don't let me drown" and engulfed me in her mouth. I pulled her up from beneath the water.

"Not here. There are too many people. Let's go to your room," I panted.

"Put a towel around you otherwise all the women here will want to come back to my room with us," she giggled.

Claudette put on her robe and led me by the hand to her room. She dragged me through the door and pinned me to the wall. Her robe slipped off her shoulders and fell to the floor, together with my trunks. There was no turning back now. It had all happened so quickly and my willpower was non-existent. We finished up having sex in her bed, both drenched in sweat, me riddled with guilt. Lying on our backs looking up at the ceiling, Claudette moved onto her side to pour us both a glass of champagne.

"I've waited a long time for that, Bubs, but it was worth it," she purred. "You have a lot of bruising on your body, face and hands. What have you been up to?"

"Your twins and some of their mates attacked me and killed my dog."

"Oh, my God!" She said, placing her hand over her mouth. "The vicious bastards."

"You've mentioned something to someone about the robbery. What have you said and to whom? No lies, Claudette, I need to know the truth." I stared into her eyes.

"Oh, God," she said again. "The guy I'm with is an old school friend of the boys and one night he knocked me around a bit, pressing me about Charlie's death. I broke down and told him about the robbery. No names and I didn't say that you or I were involved, or how much money. I just said it was a couple of Charlie's mates. They are guessing who was involved." She began to cry.

"They say they'll go to the police if they don't get five million in cash. Will they?" I asked.

"They all have form, including my boyfriend, Terry Nash, so I doubt it. It's violence they've done time for. They all think they're above the law and superior to everyone. I only went with Terry because he is young and fit. He's sort of a trophy boyfriend when we go out." Claudette was blowing her nose and wiping her eyes as she told her story.

"I know the expression blood is thicker than water, but do you have anything on these boys that we could use as leverage against them?"

"I have no bond with those boys, they are the dregs. And as for Nash, well, I would like to see the back of him for good. The three of them run some sort of protection racket in the West End, and Terry gets drugs from Europe and they employ people to sell them to kids in the clubs. The police have been round on more than one occasion to my house looking for them. They even came with a warrant to search my place, even though they don't live with me."

"Do you know of any contacts they work with or enemies they may have? I know this might be difficult, but your life and future lie in their hands," I said with some compassion.

"Nash talks about Freddie Forsyth a lot, but I don't know anything about him. And Bill Sullivan hates the boys. He claims they got him put away." Claudette looked drained and, without her mask of makeup and lipstick, vulnerable. I felt sorry for her. A life with Charlie knocking her around and now this bloke, Nash, doing the same. You could argue that her type court this type of man, but even if that were true, no woman deserves that amount of disrespect and violence.

I got out of bed, put my tracksuit back on and left without saying another word.

I drove back to Blackheath. The country lanes and kites flying overhead had none of the previous attraction to me. I was disgusted with myself for having sex with Claudette, for the mess we were in and the danger these three hoodlums were causing to me, my family and my friends. I was in no mood to buy a gun. I just felt fucking angry.

CHAPTER FIVE
THE ELEPHANT IN THE ROOM

It was twelve o'clock on Friday and Todd and I were on our way to the Blacksmiths Arms to meet the guys for a debrief on the previous week's activities. I needed to speak to Michael, who had been there for me at the Heath, but I had no time until later tonight or tomorrow.

I pulled into the pub car park with Bet behind me and made my way inside to join the guys. Pepper and Slippery looked settled and had probably been there since the doors opened. I'd not invited Claudette for obvious reasons.

"Hi, guys, great to see you. 'H', you look well. A Peroni and whatever the guys and Bet want. And one for yourself too, 'H'. So, here we are at the old haunt. I'm keen to find out what we know about the arseholes." I passed Bet a gin and tonic, gave her a wink and squeezed her arm as a silent thank you for being there for me at the Heath. She smiled back knowingly. Bet had lost weight and my first thought was that there must be a new guy on the scene. It's a tell-tale sign.

Todd spoke first. "I went to the twins' old college on the pretext of sending my kids there. I told them that Claudette had recommended the school as her two boys had boarded there. The principal's reaction was one of surprise. She pointed out that the boys had not achieved anything, academically. They certainly weren't model pupils. In fact, she was very surprised that their mother had recommended the college as neither she nor her husband had attended a single parents' evening or any of the rugby matches the boys played in. The principal was coy about giving out any further information about the twins. At the end of her talk about the college's achievements and some of the pupils who had gone on to become politicians, writers and recognised academics, I came away with the feeling that my kids would have no chance of being accepted there because of my affiliation to the family.

"When I left her office, I came across a janitor. He's probably called something different but you get my drift. I asked him about the twins and he was much more vocal. He told me that those two, and a boy called Terry Nash, were a nightmare, always bullying other boys and jumping on any teacher who had any weakness they could exploit.

"He said all three were expelled for torturing another pupil, whose life they made a misery. They took money from him in exchange for not beating him any more than they were already. A month after they left, he committed suicide. Although the whole episode was quietly swept under the carpet for the sake of the college's reputation, they all knew who was to blame. The janitor hated all three of them and knew he had spoken too freely to me. It's possible he was a victim of their cruelty and just wanted to offload," Todd concluded.

"Putting the squeeze on people for money seems to be a habit they can't shake off. What about the boyfriend? Pepper, Slippery, any news there?" I asked

"Yes, his name is Terry Nash. He's a school mate of the twins, as Todd described. He's done time for grievous

143

bodily harm against a small-time drug dealer from Peckham, and the word is he's a spiteful shit who thinks he's it around south London. He takes Claudette out occasionally, but not when he's doing business with the twins. All three are making a name for themselves around that manor as a firm that is not to be messed with. But there is no respect for them amongst local villains, who can't stand them. They don't drink or socialise in the manor. They just come in and out on business," said Pepper, with Slippery nodding in agreement at his side.

"Anything to add, Bet?" I asked.

"No, luv. They sound like up-and-coming gangsters trying to make their mark in the manor. I don't know none of 'em," said Bet with contempt.

"Okay," I said. "I met with Claudette." Just saying her name brought back flashes of our sexual encounter. "She says she has no time for the twins. She never brought them up. She wasn't a mother to them and they hate her. As for the boyfriend, he knocks her about, and during one of those sessions he put the squeeze on her about the robbery and Charlie's murder. She claims she gave no names, just said it was some of Charlie's mates and maybe it was one of them who killed him for his loot. She implied that it is all guesswork, and him and the twins know nothing beyond that. They have no idea that she was in on the heist or that she got any money from it. They're just flying a kite to see how things shake out. She confirmed they were into extortion and drugs with a bloke called Freddie Forsyth, but there is another face on the manor called Bill Sullivan who cannot stand the twins. She claims to know no more than that."

"I know Freddie," said Bet. "He runs a drug racket in south London and pulled my Wolfy for muscle from time to time. If they are running with him, it's heavy duty stuff going down."

"I know Bill Sullivan. I shared a cell with him in Wandsworth," explained Pepper. "He was in for dealing but always claimed he never got involved with drugs and he was set up to get him away from the south London scene. He's all right, is Billy. If he hates the twins, he's worth a tug."

"Good work, guys. We now need a plan of action we all buy into, and we've got to move as soon as possible. The twins gave me a month to come up with the five million, but they will never wait that long before they come after me. We have to decide if we include Claudette in all this or if it's too risky. And we need to agree on how likely it is that the twins will go to the police. Do we pay them off or call their bluff? I'm open to all suggestions."

Todd spoke up. "I think Pepper's right. We need to contact Bill Sullivan and confirm his hatred of the twins. That way we can use him as an ally in our plan. I also think we should be careful with Claudette. After all, they're her sons and, when push comes to shove, whose side will she favour? I don't think we should pay them, but if we involve outsiders, we have to have a story away from the pearls as to why we are gunning for the twins and Nash."

Slippery added his views. "We have to show some violence as they hit Bubbles. If we don't retaliate they'll think we're weak. I say we pick off this Nash bloke and teach him that we're not to be messed with. No way give them any money. They'll keep coming back for more."

Pepper was next to speak, "I think the twins need to be taught the same lesson as Nash. Let's use Claudette to set up the hit on the twins – it will confirm where her loyalties lie. And I agree with everyone. No money to the twins."

"Bet, anything to add?" I asked.

"Yes. If any or all of the three needs to be removed permanently, I'll do it. The demons are with me every day because of what I did to Charlie, so killing again won't matter."

We all burst out laughing and gave a group hug to our Bet. Wolfy would be proud of her.

"Let's hope it doesn't come to that, but thanks, Bet," I said and kissed her full on the lips, which she immediately wiped off. She was no Claudette.

"So, what's the bogus story we tell Bill Sullivan to keep any thoughts away from the pearl robbery?" I asked.

"Pepper knows Billy so he can go to see him and tell him he heard through a contact in the police that Nash and the twins are grassing up local villains to the Old Bill. If he wants revenge, he can help us teach them a lesson," said Slippery.

Todd spoke up. "Why do we need other people to get involved? It increases the risk to us. Why can't we just take care of them ourselves?"

"But doesn't that increase the risk to us?" said Pepper. "Why can't we give the job to someone else? That way, none of us gets our hands dirty. We could even take a contract out on them. The Old Bill will just put it down to drugs or turf wars."

My head was starting to feel fuzzy as I contemplated the best way forward. Were our solutions too drastic and overly complicated? Or were they too simple and not cunning or creative enough? Should we keep it within the team or outsource certain actions to others? I was struggling in my mind to take ownership and lead, but I needed to step up before it became a free-for-all of ideas. I decided to address the team.

"We were fantastically successful in the pearl robbery. Five years have passed and not a sniff from the Old Bill or any insurance people, or the banks about the large sums of money deposited offshore. Here we are with our first major problem and we mustn't panic. We need to be smart."

"The elephant in the room is the twins and Nash. But you can't eat an elephant in one go – it needs to be digested in bitesize chunks. So, from our ideas today, I propose the following. We use a strategy of fear, uncertainty and doubt, with the objective of ridding us of the twins and Nash. The fear is us hitting all three hard and violently. Uncertainty – continuing to say that we had no involvement in the robbery or Charlie's death. And their inability to come up with facts to support their assumption will cement the doubt they have of securing five million pounds from us.

"Tactically, we start the process with Pepper reacquainting himself with Billy Sullivan and planting the seed that the twins and Nash are grassing. Then assessing if Billy is chomping at the bit to fill them in, as we may need a bit more muscle.

"I will see Claudette and ask her to find out through her boyfriend the details of their whereabouts over the next week so we can plan our hit. At the same time, I'll be able to establish whether she's one of us or not. If she comes good, we'll have to get her out of her house and somewhere safe as it won't take long for them to point the finger at her.

"I don't want to do any more than that at this stage. It's important that our names and faces are unknown to the twins. We can go through the finer points of the hit when Pepper updates us on his chat with Billy. I suggest we book into the Selsdon Park Golf Club as a group and use that as our base. We'll be active over the next week and, as lovely as the Blacksmiths Arms is, the cover of four blokes and a girl at a golf hotel should work. I'll book the hotel tomorrow for a week, so bring any clubs you may have. I think I've incorporated most of your suggestions. We have a plan; our tactics may change over time but we have begun the process. I'll book us in as the Elephant Golf Society."

CHAPTER SIX
IT'S COMPLICATED

We stayed for an hour or two for the customary drink up. Bet asked to have a chat with me privately before I left for home.

"Everything okay, Bet?" I enquired.

"Not really, Bubs. I was diagnosed nine months ago with bowel cancer and it has spread to my pancreas. I've undergone chemo but nothing much is changing. I get very tired and I've lost three stone. I decided to stop any further treatment and just let nature take its course. I have no more tears to shed and it has been a lonely time without Wolfy by my side. I can stay at the hotel, but the guys will soon realise that I'm sick as I sleep so much and I don't want sympathy," she said with a vacant look in her eyes.

"Oh, Bet, I'm so sorry, I wish I'd known. Susie and I could have supported you. Don't worry about the hotel, or anything else for that matter."

"No, I want to be there. The company, the laughter – I've missed it so much. Standing drinking with you guys, you all remind me of my Wolfy and his big ugly mug. He had a softness that you guys never saw, but I will be with him soon and that gives me comfort."

I wanted to say to her, be upbeat and optimistic for the future, don't give up, there's always hope. But the words wouldn't come out. I pulled her towards me and held her tight. I could feel her bony body. Her bike leathers had been disguising the weight loss.

"Is there anything I or any of us can do for you?" I asked.

"Yes. All be yourselves and don't treat me any differently. Let the boys know and I'll see you tomorrow at the hotel. Without golf clubs."

She turned away and I headed towards the car, picking up Todd on the way. I told Todd immediately, but the others would have to wait until tomorrow. I was too upset to break the news in the pub.

After much discussion with reception over package prices for golfers, I booked the hotel. I told them we needed bed and breakfast only because we would be playing other courses in the area so no sweat about tee-off times.

I felt emotionally drained. The twins, Bet's cancer and the nonsense with Claudette were all pitching for priority in my brain. But despite feeling sorry for myself, I needed to see Michael. He'd been there for me, so I called him and we agreed to meet at the local pub at eight that evening. I lay on the bed and was asleep within a few minutes. An hour later, I woke up, showered, threw some clothes in an overnight bag, got my clubs and golf shoes from the garage and put them in the boot of the car. I was all ready for the morning.

I headed off to the pub. Michael was up at the bar with his right hand wrapped around a straight glass with a pint of his favourite bitter.

"What you having, Bub. Peroni?"

"No, I'll have the same as you for a change. How has your day been, Michael?"

"Same old, same old. I get bored at that place. It lacks excitement," he said turning to me. "Not like your life, Bubs!"

"Well, there's a lead in if ever there was one. Thanks for being at the Heath for me. I wanted to thank you earlier but life has been a little hectic. Not boring and not lacking in excitement either. Cheers," I said as we chinked glasses and drank.

"What's going on, Bubs? You don't have to tell me but maybe, just maybe, I might be able to help. Francesca has not seen Susie or the kids at school. If you're in trouble, let me help."

I knew I was taking a big risk, but I decided to tell Michael everything. If my gut instinct that he was a good 'un was wrong then we could include him with the twins to receive some special treatment, but deep down I knew that wouldn't be necessary. He had proved himself to be more than a sunny weather friend. It took me forty-five minutes and three pints to tell him the whole story. The only bits I left out were the names of our firm and my sexual tangle with Claudette.

Michael was shaking his head with a wry smile on his face as he acknowledged the fact that he was drinking with the leader of a gang that had pulled off the biggest robbery of all time in the UK.

"So, Michael, I'm not sure how you can help me but I've given you the burden of knowing something that you can never tell anyone. Not Francesca, your dad or anyone. At some stage I'll need to tell the gang that you know, but not yet. Your help may be best used if you're in the shadows. I'll sort some money out for you as any role you provide unfolds. Is that okay?"

"Sure," said Michael, who seemed lost for any more words beyond that.

"Let's have one more drink," I said, "then I must move on and leave you to digest what you now know. I respect your opinion, Michael, so if I've missed a trick or you have alternative solutions to the pickle we find ourselves in, let me know."

"I will do, Bubs. I want you to know that my lips are sealed and if there's anything you want me to do, I'm here for you. It's probably a good time for me to tell you about my dad. As you overhead that old tart say, he's in Belmarsh Prison. He got sent down for ten years.

"He's a habitual criminal and has been in and out of nick for the last thirty-five years. This time it was for a bank job. He's got less than a year of his sentence left to do. Mum despairs of him, but she knew who she married and always has him back when he comes out of the nick, pleading with her that he has learnt his lesson and never again. As she says to me, 'I love him and that's that!'"

"And you, Michael, have you ever trod that path?" I asked.

"Not really. A little bit of juvenile stuff but, seeing the heartache it brought my mum and standing in the gallery watching my dad being sentenced like some low-life, it was never for me."

"So, why offer up your services now. What's changed?" I asked.

"I really don't know. Maybe because of you and our friendship, the money I may get for helping out, boredom in my job, seeing your big house compared to my small semi, the excitement and the thrill of danger... I'm not sure why but I just know I'm prepared for what may lie ahead. I have the nous and balls to see it through. Why did you take the leap to do the biggest robbery on record? What motivated you?" said Michael, flipping the spotlight from him to me.

I gave a big grin, paused for a good few seconds and looked him straight in the eyes.

"I really don't know."

We both wrapped our arms around one another in a hug and laughed our heads off.

We then spotted Janice and her wing woman walking into the pub, continuing their search for two Mr Corporates. It was our cue to leave. We strolled back to our respective homes, discussing along the way the options for removing the twins and the boyfriend. I could almost see the cogs whirring in Michael's brain, deliberating the possible solutions.

"There is one thing you can do for me. Tomorrow at twelve thirty, call me on my mobile. I'll answer, but once I have, hang up."

"Sure," said Michael.

I called Pepper and Slippery and told them about Bet. I explained that she still wanted to meet at the golf club as planned and see the situation to its conclusion. I then telephoned Susie on her mobile and took a chance and said come home with the kids. I missed them all and wondered if, when Susie saw me, she would know immediately that

I'd been unfaithful to her. It was the first time since we'd met that I'd strayed. But once or twenty times, it was still wrong and I knew it.

The next day I called Claudette to meet and discuss the plan to hijack the twins and Nash. She was still at Champneys. It was her last day there but she was more than happy for me to come and see her, no doubt hoping for seconds.

CHAPTER SEVEN
THOSE THAT LIVE BY THE SWORD
DIE BY THE SWORD

I was back at Champneys asking at reception for Claudette. The girl recognised me and telephoned up to her room. The receptionist told me to go to room 237, saying "I think you know the way, sir," with a cheeky grin.

The door was open so I entered to be greeted by Claudette laying spread-eagled on the bed in a white lacy bodice accompanied by a whip, handcuffs and a cut-down feather duster, a can of whipped cream and a bowl of strawberries.

"How lovely to see you again, Bubbles. Boy, have I got some plans for you on this fine day. Come over here, come on big boy, come to Mummy."

I sat on the bed, removed my shoes and turned to her.

"Before we begin this epic adventure of cleaning and preparing for the Great British Bake Off, I want to discuss my secondary reason for coming to see you. Let's get the business done first, then we can have some fun," I said, slowly unbuttoning my shirt.

"Oh, Bubs, you're such a tease. Go on then, you naughty boy."

I felt like I was in a Carry On film. She was Barbara Windsor and I was Sid James.

"Claudette, I need to know in advance when and where the twins and Nash are going to be together without an army of their cronies around."

"Oh, that's easy. Nash always meets them on a Thursday at twelve o'clock at their flat in Marylebone and then they go by cab to a sleazy dive in Vauxhall called the Pink Pussy. I don't know the street, but they spend the afternoon there with the gay crowd. Nash says he only goes there because the twins like it. The twins are gay, but I think Nash probably swings both ways."

"What's their address in Marylebone?"

"Rathbone Court, near the station, but I don't know what number. Come on, Bubs, that's enough now, come here and give me a kiss. We were both a bit rushed before. Let's have some lovely sexy fun. All afternoon," said a pouting Claudette.

As I started to take off my jeans, my mobile rang. "Just a second, Claudette. Let me take this call and then brace yourself, girl, because I'm coming for you."

"Hello… Yes, that's me… Oh, my God, I'll be there in an hour… Is she conscious?… Thank heavens, I'm on my way."

"What's happened?" Exclaimed Claudette.

"It was the school, my daughter has had a fall and the ambulance has taken her to the local hospital. She passed out. It's a head injury. I must go, darling, I'm so sorry," I said, pulling my jeans up while putting my shoes back on at the same time.

"Not as sorry as I am," said Claudette as she crossed her arms and twisted her lips in disappointment.

Great timing from Michael, exactly twelve thirty. I left Champneys quicker than a rat up a drainpipe, but I had all the information I needed from Claudette, so next stop was home to see my lovely family.

Susie was very inquisitive about why she had gone to her mother's and checked whether everything was safe for her at home. I reassured her as best I could, explaining again that it was just a precaution after my attack and that everything was fine and maybe an overreaction on my part. The kids were excited to be home and looking forward to going back to school and seeing their friends. Susie had a moan that I hadn't put the vacuum over the carpets and there were empty mugs and dirty plates all over the house. I apologised and, not wanting to linger on the subject of my housekeeping skills, I changed the subject, suggesting a Thai takeaway tonight to save her cooking. When the kids went to bed, we could download a movie and have a catch-up chat. She gave me a faint smile and accused me of being an old charmer. More like an old liar. Lying was happening more often now and I did not like myself for it.

I stayed at home for a couple of hours and messed around with the kids, who had only been away for a week but still seemed more grown-up. Susie was blitzing the house clean, but I now had to break the news to her that Todd and I were spending a few days with the boys on a golfing break in Surrey. It had totally slipped my mind when I said about the evening's Thai meal and movie!

Susie was livid, complaining that we seemed to be drifting apart and leading separate lives. I went to give her a cuddle, but she just moved away, accusing me of having another woman in my life because she certainly wasn't getting any love and attention so somebody must be. She shouted at me, saying you don't work but you're never here. That I was secretive and that something was going on for all my mates and Todd to be here at the same time and that no doubt she would be the last person to know what was happening.

I apologised and said that since the incident on the Heath I had been a bit distant and after the golf break I would make it up to her. She wasn't impressed and told me to fuck off. So, I did and called Todd from the car, asking him what his expected time of arrival at the hotel was. He confirmed he'd be there in twenty minutes.

I pulled into the hotel car park, leaving my clubs in the boot, and checked in at reception. Room 33 on the ground floor. As I opened the room with my door card, I was half expecting to see Lenny Henry snuggled up in bed. The room had all the luxury of a Premier Inn. The best thing was the kettle, a few teabags, coffee and a couple of gingernut biscuits. The mattress was the thickness of three packs of fag papers. The solution was to get enough alcohol down my neck so that when bedtime came, I would just pass out.

I made my way to the bar and was greeted by the guys and Bet. I was desperate for a good laugh and to relax. Slippery was holding court as I walked up and took possession of my Peroni.

"So, I'm at the lights next to this white van," said Slippery, "and there's two geezers with turbans on wearing paint-stained decorators' bibs and braces. The lights change and they move ahead of me and I could read what's written on the side of the van. FAMILY DECORATORS. YOU'VE HAD THE COWBOYS NOW TRY THE INDIANS!"

I fucking laughed my head off.

"Hello, Bubs."

"Here you go, Bet, get that down your neck. No one's driving tonight so you can have a good drink."

I gave Bet a cuddle and I could tell that the boys were not treating her any differently after the news of her illness. That's just how she wanted it to be. But poor Bet looked worn out and half her original weight.

"How is everyone. You okay, Pepper?" I enquired.

"Yeah, rocking thanks, Bub. I've got some info for you and the boys when you're ready."

"And me for you. But let's have a bit of a session first, then we can talk shop."

"It's bloody freezing in this country," said Slippery. "Me and Pepper went down the Den to watch Millwall. Neither of us have brought the right clothes to wear. The team played well but the pies were just as bad as I remember and the crowd seemed a bit more yuppyish. It's not the fortress it used to be when teams hated playing us at the Den. We could get wingers substituted at half time because they couldn't stand the abuse. There wasn't many away supporters to wind up either."

"Didn't stop you getting into a row though did it," Pepper said with a grin.

"Well, the geezer was out of order. Telling me to curb my swearing... the tart.

"Yeah, but you didn't have to tell him you would fucking fill him in if he said another word."

"It's a Millwall counselling session! It's the working man's relief valve going down there and venting all your frustrations of the week," explained Slippery.

"That's as maybe but you haven't done a day's work for years so what's your excuse?"

"When I saw my anger management shrink he said it was good for me to go down there and let off steam," said Slippery with a huge grin on his face.

I caught Bet out of the corner of my eye having a good old laugh, probably thinking about her Wolfy and how much he would have loved being out with the lads.

After another hour of laughter and general childishness we moved away from the bar to a table away from the other drinkers.

"How did it go with Sullivan?" I asked Pepper.

"I met him at his local boozer. He fucking hates those twins all right. I dropped into the conversation that word was they were grassing people to the Old Bill then sat back and listened to him tell me, at length, how they were the grasses that put him away."

"I said that me and a few mates were looking to fill them in and their sidekick mate Nash. He didn't need any encouragement in offering his services, just said to let him know when and where. I didn't give any names but he's on board big time."

"Well done, Pep. So, my meeting with Claudette went well. I have the twins' address but not their flat number yet. They go to a gay club in Vauxhall called the Pink Pussy, all three of them. Regular time and day of the week. They meet at the flat around twelve before getting a taxi across to the club. Claudette gave up the info without batting an eyelid." I looked towards the boys for a reaction to the news.

Todd, the thinker, was the first to respond.

"We don't know anything about the layout of this club or how many faces are likely to be there. Or the security muscle. Five of us, excluding Bet but including Sullivan, going after three of them, minimum, as they'll have mates there, gay or not. It could be carnage, we could even be outmuscled. My thoughts are, hit them in or near their flat. We can watch the place for a while. That way we'll know how best to do it.

"Why can't we hit them outside the club after they've arrived in the cab?" asked Bet.

"Do we need more of Sullivan's heavies to make sure we're not outnumbered?" said Pepper.

"We could give all the info and use Sullivan and his firm to kill them all without us. Bung him a few bob and then none of us are involved," said Slippery. This surprised me because if there is violence involved he's normally first in the queue to dish it out, not delegate.

"Nobody is getting killed. We just need to give them a heavy beating to teach this little crowd a lesson they'll remember. That way they'll be frightened enough not to want to come back at a later date," I said.

"It's not enough. They'll be back and twice as aggressive, wanting revenge and money. Kill 'em," shouted Slippery, but not loud enough for anyone outside of our group to hear.

"I'm up for killing them as well," said Bet with a breathless voice. "Like Slippery says, it's like treading in dog shit on your shoes. You won't be able to shake them off. They'll stay around for the money and still be back for more."

"Okay, okay," I shouted. "Let's all take five. I like the idea of hitting them in or outside the cab away from the club, but I'm still not happy with all this talk of killing. I want to bring another person in as muscle, which improve the odds for us, with six to their three. It won't be one of Sullivan's goons, but someone I know and trust. The cab driver who picks them up will be one of my old taxi buddies. He'll be parked up outside the address so he'll be the first to react when they hail a cab. Don't go roughing him up as I will need to drop him a few bob in case the Old Bill want to interview him after the tear up."

I continued as nobody had responded. "The Underground at Marylebone Station is a few hundred yards from where we're planning on hitting them, so we could split up and take the tube. Otherwise we are in to nicking a couple of cars, hiding them until the day, disposing of them after the event and burning them to remove any traces of DNA. We'd have to recruit one or two drivers and run the risk of the West End traffic slowing down our getaway. It all seems cleaner to me if we cover our faces and head for the train station or walk away and grab cabs as there will be CCTV at Marylebone."

"What are we carrying for this tear up? Bearing in mind we are coming, and maybe going, on the tube," said Pepper.

"Coshes and blades, but no guns," I insisted.

"But they may be tooled up," said Slippery.

"They may be, but I doubt it as they are just going for their weekly drink at the gay club. There's no reason for them to be tooled up," I explained.

"Where exactly will we hit them in the taxi, Bub?" asked Todd.

"Dorset Square is just up from the station, but it has reduced traffic. I don't think there are any cameras, but I'll have to check that. We can stop the cab on the north corner, which is opposite the Dorset Square Hotel. Same as the hoist – we hit them the same. Noisy, fast and hard, leaving them sprawled across the cobbles while the cabby drives off. I'll do a recon of the area so we can take our positions at eleven thirty on Thursday as they leave at twelve noon for the club. Wear dark clothes with a hat or cap and a scarf that can be wrapped around your face.

"When we're done, let's get out of town. Todd, you go back to Bahrain and the boys to Spain. I'll pay off my man, who is providing the muscle. Pepper, you can pay off Sullivan and brief him on all the details. Tell him no guns and to keep his mouth shut. We'll give them ten grand each for their help and their silence. The hired hands can drag the twins out of the cab and I will take the boyfriend. Then we can bash the shit out of them. All happy? Any questions?

"I'll see you all at breakfast for a full English, but after that we can make a move home unless it suits you to stay here. If we meet at nine o'clock, we can go over anything in the plans that needs to change."

I made my way up to my room in the lift with Bet, who looked done in.

"You okay, Bet? You look tired, my sweet."

"Yeah, I'm ready for the sack. I'm sorry I didn't contribute much or that I won't be there on Thursday. To be honest, I don't feel I have the strength to lift a twig," she said breathlessly.

"You don't need to worry about a thing, Bet. You get some sleep and I'll see you in the morning."

We both got out of the lift on the second floor and slowly walked along to our respective rooms. I kissed Bet on the cheek and swiped the card to enter my room as Bet ponderously made her way along the corridor with her head bowed like a prisoner going to meet the hangman. My heart went out to her.

I lay on the bed and checked the time: ten forty. Susie may be in bed but the phone is next to it so I decided to call and hope she wasn't in a deep sleep.

"Hi, hun, it's me. I hope I didn't wake you."

"No, I wasn't asleep, but the kids have all gone off. You okay?"

"Miss you. I'll be home tomorrow, early evening. We will have had a couple of rounds of golf by then – that's enough for us all. We're not keen golfers, but it's been a laugh. I was thinking, we've not been getting on lately, and if your mum could have the kids then perhaps we could go abroad for a few days. What do you think, darling?" Listening to myself I sounded pathetic.

"I'm so unhappy. Ever since the incident on the Heath you've been so distant and secretive. The dog has gone and I feel all alone in this big house. I'm not sure going away is the answer. I can't talk anymore. I'll see you tomorrow," she said between sobs.

I needed to get home and spend time with Susie and the kids. It was a bleak time for me and I was in a dark place, but things were about to get much worse.

CHAPTER EIGHT
WISHING FOR THE PAST

I had breakfast with the boys and checked on Bet as she was not there at nine. Reception told me she had already checked out of her room. She probably couldn't wait to get back to the regular surroundings of her home. I made a mental note to visit Bet and stay in contact more, but after retribution day on Thursday.

I left the lads. Slippery and Pepper were staying at the hotel and were planning to fly out of Heathrow on the seven o'clock flight on Thursday evening. Todd was going to see his in-laws so I made my way to Shoreditch to have a cup of tea at the taxi drivers' café and speak to my mate Harry, an old school cabby who moaned continuously and always seemed to be working. He should have been a wealthy man, but he had a gambling problem and gave most of his earnings to William Hill, the bookmakers. A man of habit, I knew at this time of day he would be poring over the form guide in the *Racing Post*, circling his horses and writing the details onto a betting slip of which he had many, occasionally sipping from his cup of tea, which would be stone cold.

"Hello, you old git," I said as I sat down beside him.

"Fuck me, it's money bags come straight from the lottery to share his winnings with his old mate Harry."

"You may not be far from the truth there, Harry."
After swapping pleasantries about our respective families,
I took Harry's arm and drew him round to make sure I had
his full attention.

"Listen, Harry. I want you to do me a big favour and
I will give you five big ones for you to spend on the gee-
gees. Interested?" I asked. My eyes never left his.

"If by big ones you mean five grand, I'm all ears,"
said Harry as he broke into a smile, revealing his crooked
discoloured teeth. I had never seen him smile before and I
never wanted to see him smile again. They were like a
NAAFI piano: one black, one white, one missing.

"I want you to pick up a fare from three guys in
Marylebone, who will flag you down and ask to go to the
Pink Pussy gay club over at Vauxhall. Drive them as far as
Dorset Square, where you will be flagged down by six
people, who will drag those arseholes out of the cab and
onto the cobbles, where they will teach them a lesson that
will stop them ever interfering with little children again."

"Fucking paedophiles? The dirty bastards," snarled
Harry.

"They've got it coming to them, Harry. You've got
grandchildren. How would you feel? "I said shaking my
head in disgust.

"What do I do, Bubbles? Just say."

"Only what I've told you. You need to be outside
Rathbone Court by Marylebone Station with your For Hire
sign on. When you see them, make sure no other cabs get
to them first. Then take the route via Dorset Square, where
they will be met by the welcoming committee. Once
they've been dragged out of the cab, drive on and don't

look back. You saw nothing and you know nothing. If there are no repercussions for all those concerned, then after a month I'll give you another five grand. We need these people off our streets for our little ones to be safe."

"You can count on me, Bubs, they're filth. I'll be there."

"Here's the first five grand, Harry." I passed the cash to him under the table inside a brown envelope. "I know you won't let me down. Or the little ones' parents. We're counting on you Harry. As long as you don't tell a soul about this arrangement or talk about any of the violence that takes place on the day, another five will be yours also."

I rose to get up and leave and was not sure if Harry was going to stand and salute as he shook my hand vigorously and said, "Let's get the bastards."

I drove to Marylebone to do a reconnaissance on Dorset Square. There were no surveillance cameras, which was essential for our safety, and the hotel windows were mainly obscured by the trees so the possibility of a guest spotting us was limited. I calculated that we could stand chatting to one another in pairs at spaces of twenty yards along the road that Harry would take. This equated to two thirds of one side of the square. Travelling time on foot back to the station was four minutes. This was our most vulnerable time because there would be CCTV at the station, it would be lunchtime when we hit the twins and there could be lots of people in the streets. Nevertheless, I felt confident about the plan as I made my way home to see Susie and the kids before bedtime, but not before briefing Michael that he was on the firm, where he needed to be and what was expected of him on the day.

I arrived home around five o'clock and the kids went mad to see me, which I loved. I couldn't say I got the same reception from Susie, who headed to the kitchen to get some pasta from the walk-in larder. I wasn't looking for a row, especially not in front of the kids, so I went and sat down in the lounge so they could update me on their news since I'd last seen them. They looked so beautiful – more like their mum than me.

We watched a bit of telly, ate together and then the kids were bathed and I put them to bed looking like two angels in their PJs, with their not totally dry hair and sleepy eyes. So innocent and loving, unlike their dad, who was a thief, a liar and an unfaithful husband who was about to deliver grievous bodily harm to three guys on the cobbled streets of London. Six years ago I was a black cabbie, grafting every day, dabbling in a bit of mischief but nothing like what I have become today. And all for a pound note. Really, that's what this all boils down to, nicking some dough – well, a lot of dough – and trying to protect what I have without doing porridge for the next twenty-five years. I hated myself. Even when I shaved in the mornings I tried not to look at myself for too long as I didn't like what I saw.

Now I was about to try and pacify the love of my life, who would be happier in the three-bed semi we lived in before, with a black cab parked up in front of the house and no money to speak of but as happy as two pigs in shit and respect for a husband who was turning into Bill Sykes from *Oliver Twist*.

I broke the ice. "Would you like a drink, Susie, now the kids are asleep? There's some cold Sauvignon Blanc in the fridge."

"I think I deserve one living with you," she said without looking at me. She continued to rearrange the cushions on the sofas.

As I handed her the glass, I held onto her other hand and pulled her towards me.

"I'm so sorry for the way I've been lately. I love you more than anything, you know that. It's been a difficult time recently and I didn't give myself enough time to recover from that beating, which has not helped my frame of mind either. Let's take ourselves abroad for a few days and get ourselves back on track and let me try and make up for the way I have been towards you."

"You've been so distant and that's when you've been here. Then there's your gallivanting. You don't seem to be the same person I fell in love with. I can't remember when we last made love. To be honest, I don't think I want you near me. I just want my life to be like it was before, with you, the man I loved, respected and who cared and protected me. Now I'm like a bundle of nerves, worried for my safety and the kids. What's happening to us?" Susie burst into tears as her words trailed off into continual sobs.

"It will all be different, Susie, I promise. Come here and let me hold you. No more tears. I love you so much. We have such a beautiful family. We were so solid and will be again. Let's go off to Paris or Rome for the weekend, just me and you, and have a romantic two days. Your mum can have the kids. What do you think, darling?"

"Let me think about it. But no more lies or going off to 'golf'. You don't even like golf! No more clandestine meetings with your old cronies. Call it a woman's intuition, but I know more than you think I do. Now, pour me another wine because this one didn't touch the sides."

As I took her empty glass into the kitchen for a refill I was hoping and praying that she had no idea about Thursday's planned tear up, or Claudette. I wouldn't be standing here if she did. I took a fresh glass and poured a wine for me, which I dispensed in three gulps, and then refilled both glasses and returned to the lounge, keen to change the conversation so I wouldn't have to lie any more than I had done.

"The kids look great, Susie. You do such a great job with them," I said handing her the glass.

"Stop sucking up, Bubbles, it doesn't suit you. Just go back to being yourself, please."

"Okay, let's open another bottle and have an early night. Does that sound more like me?" I said smiling for the first time in days. She knew exactly what I meant and a hint of a smile crossed her beautiful face. I knew I had lived to fight another day.

Thursday finally arrived. Susie was taking the kids to school and was planning to meet Francesca for lunch a bit later in the day. I said I had a few errands to run but told Susie I'd be home when she got back from school with the kids.

I left wearing a black raincoat, cap and a long scarf tied around my neck, which I would use to cover my face. I took the train and tube to Oxford Circus. I was planning on walking to Marylebone in case some eagle-eyed copper took to studying any CCTV footage of people arriving in the time leading up to the tear up. I was carrying a truncheon in one of the deep inside pockets of my coat and wearing gloves so that I didn't leave any prints on the handle, in case the truncheon and I parted company.

We arrived at Dorset Square at different times, but everyone was early. By eleven forty-five we were all in place, in pairs, chatting in doorways or anywhere that was inconspicuous.

Twelve o'clock came and went. At twelve fifteen there was still no sign. I was beginning to think the worst. Claudette had tipped them off that she'd told me they always leave for the Pink Pussy at twelve or Harry had bottled it and another cabbie was taking them. We were all getting twitchy, looking up and down the road to see if I would be calling the whole thing off.

At 12.25 a back cab turned into the square. I could see it was Harry but couldn't make out who was in the back of the cab. Michael and Sullivan stepped into the road and put their hands up to stop Harry. The cab doors were flung open on both sides of the cab and the boys were laying into the occupants with their truncheons flying. As the rest of us arrived, the passengers were dragged out onto the road and we all joined in the onslaught. But there were only two of them and my heart sank. It was only the twins and not Claudette's fella, Nash.

I could tell the twins had taken a terrible beating, with six of us all lining up to make our mark. The odds of six to two were further increased when I notice Harry out of his cab, putting the boot in and trying not to get hit by the flying truncheons raining in from all angles.

I told Harry to fuck off and quick, then I shouted, "stop". I bent over the lifeless bodies. Neither were conscious. "Let's go," I shouted and we all ran our separate ways, but before leaving I sprinkled some white powder over the twins in the hope that the Old Bill would see it as a drug-related incident.

I made my way through the back streets, making sure my face was covered and my head down. I never spotted any of the guys who had left the scene of the crime and were fleeing in all directions. I wondered why Nash had not turned up at the twins' flat and if this was a potential problem for us. Would the twins go to the police and name any of us? Were they alive or had we gone too far with the beating?

We had a code of no use of mobiles between any of us, but I was desperate to know if the boys had all got away safely. I arrived back at my house and started to pack a bag of clothes for Susie and me to go for a break overseas, even though she hadn't yet agreed to go. I switched on the TV and hit the news channel, which was full of the normal political banter and our obsession with the weather. The London news followed and, as I finished putting the last few bits in the suitcase, I heard the voice of a reporter at the scene of a crime in London's West End, announcing that two young men had been dragged from a taxi and beaten half to death in a violent attack. Both were in a coma and the police were asking for any eye witnesses in the Marylebone area to come forward.

I hoped that Susie would be home soon so that we could get the kids settled at her mum's and get out of the country.

The news continued with details of another incident in London where another young man in his twenties had been shot dead on the pavement outside his house by an assailant in black leathers who left the scene of the crime at speed on a high-powered motorbike. Police were again seeking any eye witnesses who may have been in the area and seen the assailant. Oh, my God, so that's why Nash wasn't in the cab. Bet? It had to be!

A spokesperson for the police talked about the escalation of gun and knife crime in the inner city and its connection with drugs. Then a politician was interviewed outside the Houses of Parliament. He was demanding more armed police on our streets to protect the law-abiding masses who have to put up with this epidemic of drug-related incidents.

I could hear the key in the door and quickly turned off the TV in the bedroom and went downstairs to help Susie with the shopping bags. My hands were trembling and grabbing the overloaded bags helped to hide the shudder that was passing through my body.

"No kids?" I said.

"They're having tea at Mum's," said Susie as she unpacked the bags.

"Are we going off for the weekend then, Susie? Is your mum having the kids?"

"I wouldn't have done a week's shop if I was planning on going away on holiday. We need some time at home together as a family, Bubbles. I can't believe that you don't see that."

I helped her put the shopping in the fridge and the larder. It was all stuff that I like. She may be pissed off with me, but her purchases were to please me, so she must still love me. Well, that was my male logic.

Todd would be heading back to Bahrain and Slippery and Pepper to Spain. I wasn't really interested in Sullivan. He just needed to keep his mouth shut. Michael was pretty much unknown to anyone other than me and Todd, who had only been given a brief summary of our friendship. So, he should be safe and an unknown if it all came on top with the Old Bill. Bet will be in hiding and seeing out her days, if she was the black leather motorbike assailant.

If either or both of the twins died as a result of the beatings, it wasn't a question of ABH or GBH, it was murder. I needed to leave town like the others, with or without Susie.

"Susie, darling. I need to get away for a bit. I know the timing is crap as I agree we need some time together – you, me and the kids. But the thing is, I've taken revenge on the arseholes that attacked me and killed our dog. I am hoping we haven't gone too far, but I need to lay low for a while until things blow over. You said no more lies so there you have it: the truth."

"Oh, Bubbles, what has happened to you? The boy I fell in love with. You've gone from a cabbie to a thief and a gangster, involved in... I don't know what... I don't know you anymore. Just go, Bubbles, and leave me to bring the kids up in peace without the fear of a knock on the door, not knowing if it's the police or thugs. Just go."

I went to hold her, but she brushed me aside. I went to speak but I just didn't know what to say. I collected my bag, new throwaway phone, charger, passport, driving licence and a shitload of cash I had hidden in the kids' bedroom.

I left the house calling out, "I love you, Susie. And tell the kids I love them too."

I jumped in the car and drove to Michael's. We had a chat in his doorway.

"You okay, Michael? Have you seen the London news?" I asked.

"Yes, and I guess the rider on the motorbike must be the person I saw on the Heath when you met the twins for the second time?" said Michael.

"You could be right, but it was all news to me when I heard it on the TV. Listen, Michael. I want you to take this money. It's one hundred and fifty thousand quid. Use it for whatever you think is in our best interest and keep an eye on Susie for me. She has plenty of money, but she will need support from Francesca as I don't know how long I'll be away for. I need to get out of this country tout suite. If either of the twins croak it or are conscious and grass and the Old Bill have any sort of lead, then the airports and ports will have my details. You should be okay, Michael. Nobody knows you or anything about you, so staying here with your family is your best option.

"I'll be in touch," I said and was about to go.

"Wait," said Michael, grabbing my arm.

"We have a group of us from De Beers going to South Africa on business in two days' time. The PA who is booking the flights, hotels and stuff has a bit of a crush on me. If I can get her to book you in with the party of eight flying out, it becomes less conspicuous for you. Just meet me at the airport and say that we know each other and happen to be staying at the same hotel. Integrated with us and the booking through the company looks to an outsider like you are part of the De Beers business trip. What do you think?"

"I like it. Can you sort the costs out and let me know the details?" I said.

"Well, I seem to have ample funds now!" Michael said with a smile.

"Okay, here's my new mobile number. I suggest you get a pay as you go mobile that you can use to stay in contact with me," I said, and this time I did turn and go.

CHAPTER NINE
ON THE RUN

To say the next few days were stressful would be an understatement. The police were all over everything and interviewing everyone. The two incidents were being linked as the twins and Nash were known to the police and, from local radio to the BBC, all were speculating about turf wars over drug distribution and drug lords. The twins were on the critical list, so at least they were still alive. On the one hand, if they both died then the case file on the pearl robbery would remain buried in the annuls of unsolved crimes at Scotland Yard. But if they died, we would be hunted down as killers. If they lived and blabbed, we would be wanted for the biggest robbery since the Hatton Garden safe deposit heist and for Actual Bodily Harm to the terrible twins. But, so far, my photo fit or any of the team had not appeared in the press or on television.

It was the day of the flight and I couldn't wait to get out of the country. I had chatted to Michael on our new phones and we agreed to meet at Heathrow in the terminal toilets, so he could give me the tickets and reservation at the hotel in Johannesburg. I asked about Susie and Michael said that she was pretty distraught but going about her business with the kids and keeping up appearances that all was well at home.

We flew out business class with British Airways and I sat in the aisle seat behind Michael. There had been no problems at customs, so I settled down to a Bloody Mary and some nibbles and craned my neck to take a look at the green hills of Blighty as who knew when I would be back, and under what circumstances.

The flight was good, although I didn't sleep much. Instead I watched two movies and thought about Susie and the kids and how I missed them already. Michael had been chatting to his work colleagues, dozing and watching the odd movie. We would wait until we were in the privacy of the hotel in Sandton, Johannesburg, before having any meaningful conversations.

The trip from the airport to the hotel was my first glimpse of South Africa and its vastness. The townships of corrugated sheds had clothes draped over washing lines and electricity cables tapped into them to provide light to the pitiful accommodation the poor blacks called home. The taxi slowed down at the red traffic lights but did not stop as gangs of men straddled both sides of the road, not in a menacing way but just hoping an open-backed truck may come along and choose one or more for a day's manual labour.

My first impressions were of poverty residing in a beautiful country. The hotel was in a sort of shopping mall, with walkways to the restaurants, shops and a square, all within an enclave of luxury and wealthy activities designed to shield the tourists in the luxury hotels from the poverty that lay outside its perimeter.

I showered and changed into blue skinny-ish jeans and a pale blue Ralph Lauren shirt with tan pointed shoes.

After a short stroll I settled on a restaurant called the Butcher, which specialised in, you guessed it, meat. The steak I ate was magnificent and the South African red wine that accompanied the meal, a grenache noir from Stellenbosch, went down like velvet. To top it all, the exchange rate of pounds to SA rand made the meal as cheap as chips.

I had a stroll and made my way back to my hotel room and into bed. I didn't sleep much that night but lay on my bed reflecting on the past events. I had left a message on Michael's hotel room answering service to meet for breakfast at six a.m. before his work colleagues came down, so we could have a chat.

Michael's time was being consumed by his work and he was not senior enough to extricate himself without permission. He would be returning to the UK the day after tomorrow, so this breakfast may be our last time together. He was my only link with home and I knew the loneliness would set in the minute he left.

Armed with a bowl of muesli and a yogurt, I made my way to a breakfast table. The restaurant didn't officially open until seven a.m., but the staff were good enough to provide a pot of coffee as Michael made his way across the restaurant to join me.

"Hi, Michael, sleep well?"

"I hate this fucking job, I'm not sure if I can stick it much longer," said Michael as he poured us both a cup of steaming hot black coffee.

"It may not be for much longer. Let's ride out this situation and then we can talk again about your future. I'm not sure if I want those twins to live or die, but it's hardly in our hands what happens.

"There are a few things I want you to do for me. Harry the taxi driver needs five grand more for keeping his mouth shut. Leave it three weeks then sit outside the taxi drivers' café in Shoreditch. When he comes out, slip him a brown envelope with the cash in but don't talk to him. Please keep an eye on Susie. I'm sure she hates me. Get Francesca to reassure her that I love her so much but don't tell her that I'm here in South Africa. Let me know via our new phones what the news is about the twins or any snippets on the Marylebone attack. I know I'm asking a lot from you, but I trust you, Michael, and the other lads are in Bahrain or Spain so can't have their ear to the ground back home."

"Nothing is a problem, Bubs. I'll take care of things back home. Try not to worry about Susie. I'll call you when I have something to report."

"Nobody knows you, Michael, so keep your head down and try and keep it that way."

"I guess this will be the last time we'll see each other for a while, but I'll be in touch soon as," said Michael as he rose from his chair and gave me a hug before heading for the hotel lift.

I could have cried as my only link with home was heading back to his room and, ultimately, the UK and Blackheath.

CHAPTER TEN
SOUTH AFRICA

Six weeks had passed and Sandton was done and dusted for me. I needed to move on somewhere. The barman at the hotel called Rodney, a South African from Kimberley, was my only contact for the whole six weeks. He was a great lad, always smiling and never asking a prying question or what I was doing in Jo'burg. He loved to talk about Chelsea and called me John Terry if his boss was out of earshot. He lived in the township with his mother, two sisters and a crippled brother. He was the only one working so his money took care of the whole family. His goal was to be voted employee of the month and to one day have a home of his own.

I tried to keep a low profile, but in the evenings the businessmen, women and tourists in the hotel were keen to talk and every conversation commenced with, 'So what brings you to Jo'burg?' A conversation I did not wish to join in with.

I asked Rodney if he could come to my room before he started his shift as there was something I wanted to discuss with him. He agreed and the next day his smiling face appeared at my door.

"Come in, Rodney. Would you like a cold drink or a coffee?" I asked.

"No thanks, John Terry," he said with a huge grin.

"Call me Bubbles from now on, Rodney. That's what my friends call me." His grin softened as if I had hurt his feelings.

"Rodney, I wish to go to Kimberley. You told me that was your hometown before working here in Jo'burg so I'm assuming you know your way around the town. Is that correct?"

"Yes," he said tentatively.

"Okay, what do you earn in a year working at the hotel?"

Rodney had a look of bewilderment on his face.

"Fifty thousand rand a year, plus tips, which I have to share with my shift managers. I don't understand why you are asking me these questions, Mr Bubbles?"

"It's just Bubbles. Because I need to spend some time in Kimberley. I need to find accommodation, a travel plan and someone to drive me around while I am there who can speak Afrikaans. I have some business to take care of while I'm there and I trust you. I'd like you to be that person, Rodney. Before you tell me about not wanting to lose your job here at the hotel, this is my offer. I will give you fifty thousand rand (approximately three thousand pounds) to give to your family while you are in Kimberley and one hundred and fifty thousand rand (nine thousand pounds) to you for the time you spend with me. How does that sound?"

"What an offer, Mr Bubbles! But how long will I be away from my mother and what do I have to do for all this money," said Rodney with his face in his hands, shaking his head.

"Six months maximum and your job will be no more than I just explained. Just drive me around, translate and find us some accommodation – maybe a bungalow in a private and secure area. I will not ask you to break the law."

We stood holding each other's stare as Rodney absorbed the proposition.

"Take your time to think about it. Discuss it with your family if you need to. Ask them to keep your conversation just between your family. If you say no, I don't want half the township at my door requesting a job. Do you understand, Rodney?"

"I do understand and I don't need to discuss with my family. I accept the job," roared Rodney, wide-eyed and jumping up and down with excitement.

"Fantastic. Tell your boss you are resigning today as you must return to Kimberley immediately as a relative is very sick and they want you back home. Tell him nothing about me or our adventure, and then come to see me as I need your help to buy a car. All right?" I said, nodding my head to help him with the decision.

"Absolutely, boss. I will come back to your room within the hour," said my new employee, whose face resembled a Cheshire Cat.

"Rodney, remember to look a little sadder when you resign as your relative is supposedly at death's door. Just give yourself ten minutes to calm yourself."

"Yes, boss."

Rodney turned and left with a skip in his stride. He must be the only person I had made remotely happy in months. His happy go lucky attitude to life was infectious and I found myself smiling at his good fortune. At least that is what I hoped it would be.

Sure enough, Rodney returned as promised. He'd told his boss in a flood of tears about his poor, ailing relative, scribbled a note of resignation and slouched out of the door without negotiating his last pay check. Why should he? Rodney was soon to be rich by township standards.

I jumped in a taxi and picked him up outside the hotel gates. We made our way to the Kia Garage, where I bought a Kia Sportage. Not too flashy, but solid and reliable. Jo'burg is not the place to break down, anywhere. That evening, Rodney said his farewells to the family and handed over the money I gave him for his mother. From Rodney's description of events, they were upset to see him go, but the sight of the cash certainly softened the blow as they vigorously waved him farewell.

I packed my bags, checked out and stopped the Sportage to collect Rodney and his battered case outside the hotel. He jumped into the driver's seat and we set off on my first experience of Rodney's driving. If you can recall the first time you got behind a wheel as a learner, kangarooing down the road, unsure of the width of your car, trying to coordinate hands, feet and brain with fear in the pit of your stomach that someone could lose a life as you were not really in control... That is how I felt alongside Rodney. It was going to be a long journey to Kimberley, the largest city and capital of the North Cape Province, and a bloody long way from south London.

CHAPTER ELEVEN
KIMBERLEY

We arrived in Kimberley and checked into separate rooms at a three-star hotel, which was more than adequate until we found a house to rent. I had taken responsibility for most of the driving once we were on the motorways as Kimberley is located at the intersection of the N12 and the N8 and Rodney's inability to concentrate was driving me nuts, which was only surpassed when he took over the navigation and I realised he didn't know his left from his right!

We ate and then turned into bed for a well-earned kip. My phone rang and it was Michael's voice that stirred me from my sleep.

"Hiya, Bubs, it's Michael. How you doing, mate?"

"Yeah, good. What's new?"

"The Old Bill have been putting pressure on the taxi driver and he's crumbling. Thing is, he only knows you and thinks it was a paedophile attack. He hasn't mentioned any names yet, but my guess is it won't be long."

"How do you know all this, Mike?"

"I had a cuppa with him down the cabbie café."

"But I told you to just slip him the money and not to talk to him."

"Sorry, Bub, I don't remember you saying that. Just trying to find out what's going on. Anyway, the twins are still in a coma and the hospital are saying that being twins it's possible if one comes out of the coma, so will the other. Susie and the kids are all okay, your mum has been over staying with them. Susie misses you. Are you still at the hotel in Stanton?"

"Yeah, yeah," I replied somewhat vaguely.

"How is the money holding out that I gave you," I asked.

"Yeah, okay I've spent a bit here and there, you know. I quit my job, I couldn't stand it anymore, so home all the time now. Go to the gym a bit, pop round yours with Francesca and have a drop of tea with Susie. Do you need me to do anything for you, Bub – contact any of the others or are you looking to come home soon? You there, Bubbles, the line's gone quiet?"

"No, I'm here, it's maybe just a poor reception or a delay on the line. Anyway, room service are at the door so must go. Stay in touch, Michael."

I switched my mobile off and reflected on the call. Michael seemed different, but I couldn't put my finger on why I felt that way. Or maybe it was just me getting paranoid, being out of the loop and relying on Michael to be my eyes and ears. I only managed a few hours' sleep, but after a shower I was ready for the day.

I decided to telephone Todd on his secure line and was pleased to hear his voice when he picked up.

"Hi, Todd, it's me."

"Oh, my God, how are you? Where are you? Mum's at yours with Susie, who is beside herself with worry"

"It's okay, Todd, I'm fine. Any update on the business at Marylebone?"

"Well, the guys in Spain got tapped up in their local bar by some guy who was asking questions they thought were a bit suspect. In the end they decided they were overreacting, but they stayed in their villas getting pissed rather than going out drinking and talking to strangers. Michael told me that the taxi driver is being grilled regularly by the Old Bill and is close to cracking."

"Michael told you? How?"

"I was round yours seeing Susie and the kids and Michael was there and said you had asked him to keep an eye on Susie. He told me about the cabbie when we were alone."

"Was Mum there? Has Michael met Mum?"

"No, no. I don't think so," said Todd. "Where are you? Are you on your own? Are you coming home to Susie and the kids soon?"

"Not at the moment, but please tell them I love them and am thinking of them. Todd, can you let Mum have this mobile number. If it's on your screen, memorise it and ask mum to call me tomorrow at eight a.m. Love you, Todd," I said, a little too emotionally.

"Don't make it sound so final. Love you, too," replied Todd.

Next thing for me was coffee with Rodney. Rodney was uneducated, couldn't drive and lacked basic skills, but his art for survival made him quick through the gate. He got things in seconds, long before the next person had, and over our breakfast confirmed my confidence in him.

"Morning, boss. It's nice for me being the customer and not the person waiting on folk in the hotel. I've been busy this morning. We have two potential house rentals to view, which my cousin has recommended. We need to be there in the hour, so after your coffee, we should go. I'll drive," said Rodney with some assertiveness. "I know the way."

The massive hole that is the Kimberley mine dominates the area. During the period from 1871–1914, fifty thousand miners dug the hole with picks and shovels, yielding nearly 3,000kg of diamonds. As we drove around the mine I visualised the African blacks employed as cheap labour by the mine owners in the stifling heat, with all those flies and no sanitation.

We pulled up outside a gated and walled perimeter. Inside stood a bungalow set in grounds with trees, a small swimming pool and a brick BBQ. There was a lady by the gate who was either the owner or from the estate agent. Rodney leapt from the car and into her arms with much screaming and laughter, which for me will always characterise our Rodney.

"Boss, please meet my cousin, Dintle."

Dintle was in her mid-twenties and a beautiful girl with the most radiant smile I had ever seen.

"Good morning, Dintle. I'm very pleased to meet you. My friends call me Bubbles."

Our eyes locked and I thought my legs would give way.

"Bubbles, what an unusual name. I am very pleased to meet you too, Bubbles. When Rodney called me I had only just received the instruction on this property, so we shall both be viewing it for the first time. The owners live in Cape Town and are looking for a long-term lease, minimum one year. I hope that fits with your plans. Let's take a look, shall we?"

I followed Dintle through the gates as far as the porch. She didn't walk, she glided, and her printed summer dress clung to her body. I was mesmerised. On the porch, Dintle pointed out the trees and shrubs, the pool and the security gates and alarms. Turning the key to enter, I was surprised at how European it looked, with cream sofas and white fabrics and curtains. The introduction of African dark wood furniture with white lace draped over the top was a welcome reminder of the country I was in. The double french doors led to a patio area and then onto the pool. The gardens were well kept and Italian statues were dotted around the flower beds.

"What do you think, Mr Bubbles, could you see yourself living here? Of course, we still have the bedrooms and bathrooms to see," said Dintle.

"How would you describe the area?"

"Upmarket, good school nearby. Lots of history in the area. Security is a must in South Africa, but there are no townships nearby. Sorry, Rodney, that is not to say that your township is full of bad people," she said. She looked at him as if peering over reading glasses, with her eyebrows raised and a gentle smile.

"Could you live here in this house, Dintle, or should we be moving on to view the next property?" I said.

"Goodness, I would never have the money to live somewhere like this. It's just beautiful. I have viewed the next house before and it just doesn't compare to this. So, my answer is yes."

There was a long pause and we just looked at each other. It was as if a thunderbolt had struck me and removed the air from my lungs and the strength from my legs.

"There are three double bedrooms, two en suites and a master bathroom and separate toilet. Shall we proceed?"

I nodded and followed the swishing dress.

The main bedroom was all white – white shutters at the windows and a white muslin mosquito net above the bed. A picture on the wall of the ocean at Cape Town showed white foam waves crashing into the shore, with the blue of the sky offering the only colour in the room. The blue was carried through into the en suite, with light blue and white striped towels to enhance the feeling of the beach and summer. It was exquisite.

We returned to the main living area and Dintle gave me the price to rent for the year, broken down into monthly payments, then looked at me for a reaction.

"Thank you, Rodney, for arranging this morning. And thank you, Dintle, and congratulations on your first sale today. I adore it."

Dintle rushed towards me and gave me an enthusiastic hug and a massive thank you before she spun around to ruffle Rodney's hair and plant a kiss on his cheek.

"Rodney and I have some things to do today so I shall be busy. But perhaps tomorrow I could take you to dinner, Dintle. Would that be okay?" I said, feeling as if my beating heart would explode from my chest.

"I would like that very much. Thank you," replied Dintle, still holding my gaze with her beautiful eyes. "If you can find your way back here, I could meet you at eight o'clock."

"Eight o'clock it is then. Until tomorrow, bye."

"Bye."

Rodney and I made our way to the car.

"Where to, boss?"

"Is your cousin married, Rodney, or is she engaged to be married? Does she live locally? What…"

Rodney interrupted before I rambled on indefinitely.

"Well, boss, there were sparks flying in the house. I think you like my cousin, and I think maybe she likes you too. No, she is not married or engaged, and yes, she lives locally with my aunt and uncle. Where will I stay if you move into the house, boss? My uncle is my mum's brother and they have not spoken to one another in years, so I cannot stay with them," said Rodney.

"You can stay with me at the house for a while, but if you drive me mad you'll have to find accommodation elsewhere."

"Thanks, boss. Do you need a cook and cleaner? I know a friend of my mother who is a wonderful cook," said Rodney.

"Possibly, but for now I want to grab a bite to eat and have a look at the mines. So, let's go and find a café close by and you can tell me all about your beautiful cousin."

We found a small café where we ate a sandwich, drank coffee ordered by Rodney in Afrikaans and I listened to him extol the virtues of Dintle from a small child, through schooling and singing in the church choir right up until today, where she works for Kimberley Real Estate with three other staff. In a dark world it seemed as though Dintle was a shining light bringing happiness to those she met. If there was friction with her family and Rodney's, there was no sign of any animosity between the two cousins.

We went on a tour of the 'hole' and I learnt more about the Kimberley mine, its past and the siege during the second Boar War. I knew nothing of the Boar War – it was never mentioned when I was at school. I only knew the film *Zulu* and Michael Caine's classic line, 'Don't point those bloody spears at me', which I am not sure he even said but became the catch phrase used to impersonate Michael Caine.

They talked about Cecil Rhodes and Barney Bernato, and how they made their fortunes and formed De Beers, the world-famous diamond house. Michael had spoken of Barnato in the pub when he was talking about his nan and recounting the story of the accident when Barnato went overboard while strolling along the deck with his cousin Solly Joel, never to be seen again. However, history tells us that Solly re-emerges a little later, named on the board of directors at De Beers.

The weather was hot and I was keen to return to the hotel for a swim and to relax. Rodney asked to borrow the car as he wanted to visit some friends and probably show off his car and 'big up' his new job. Good luck to him, I thought, as I jumped out of the car and headed to my room, leaving Rodney to his exploits.

I ate dinner at the hotel, which was okay. I ended up having an early night after lying on my bed and thinking about my dinner date tomorrow with Dintle and how beautiful she was.

Next thing I knew, I was awoken in the morning with the sound of my mobile phone, which had been programmed with a ring tone from the film *The Good, the Bad and the Ugly* – that just about summed me up. It was Mum.

"Hello, son, how are you? Are you safe?" she said, and it was comforting to hear her voice.

"Yeah, good thanks, Mum. And you, how are you keeping?"

"Good. What's going on, son? Susie is distraught and the kids don't understand where their dad is. I want answers, and don't give me any cock and bull stories," she said firmly. She always was scary, more so than my old man.

"I had to get even with those bastards that beat me up and killed my dog. They were putting the squeeze on us all for money or they would go to the Old Bill and grass us up for their dad's murder and the pearl job. We couldn't be sure if they were blagging it, so we thought we would scare them off and teach them a lesson not to mess with us.

"Their dad's murder?"

"Yes, they are Claudette's twins and her fancy man is the geezer that was killed. But I had nothing to do with Jack's death or the boyfriend's murder."

"What a fucking mess," yelled Mum. "Where are you now?"

"It's best you don't know. I am lying low and keeping an eye on the health of the twins, who are in a coma. If they snuff it, I could be hunted down for murder," I said. As I explained it all to Mum I realised just what a gigantic fucking mess it really was.

"Let me think," said Mum. "I'll call you tomorrow at the same time."

"Mum, lose that mobile and buy a throw away. Don't go after Claudette, she has helped us get to the twins. Don't do anything or talk to anyone. Certainly not Susie."

"I'll call you tomorrow."

The line went dead. This was not a problem halved but rather a problem doubled now that I had involved my mother. I had an empty feeling deep in my gut and a sense of complete loneliness. I wanted to cry, sob like a baby, but no tears came. I showered and dressed for the day.

CHAPTER TWELVE
DINTLE

Everything in Kimberley was centred around the diamond business. The cafés, shops and bus companies all carried the name of the town and that special commodity that put Kimberley on the map. I read anything and everything I could lay my hands on that would expand my knowledge of diamond mining. I found the whole thing fascinating. I dozed a little and looked forward to my dinner date with Dintle once that little tyke Rodney returns with my car after gallivanting around Kimberley showing off his new wheels.

I wasn't sure about booking a restaurant, so in the end I decided to leave it to Dintle to choose. Rodney returned with the car so I set off, slightly nervous, for my dinner date.

As I pulled up outside the house, which was soon to be mine for a year, Dintle was waiting. She was wearing a simple yellow floral print dress with a matching flower in her hair, white sandals and a small white clutch bag. The look was not London, the clothes weren't expensive or the height of fashion, but, somehow, with her white teeth contrasting with her chocolate-coloured skin, standing on the steps of the house, she looked beautiful.

As I approached, she walked towards me and kissed me gently on the cheek. She took my arm and we strolled, in step, towards the car. She was the first to speak.

"If you haven't booked anywhere I thought we might go to a restaurant not far from here that has an international menu as I wasn't sure what type of food you like. If that's okay with you?"

"Yes, that's fine," I said quietly. Somehow, she had taken my breath away. I graciously opened the passenger door for her, only to see a discarded crisp packet on the floor of the car, courtesy of Rodney, no doubt. She made no mention of it and we proceeded to the restaurant under Dintle's direction. It was small and intimate, although the décor was in need of a refresh. Nevertheless, the greeting we received was friendly and we were soon settled at our table.

"What would you like to drink, Dintle?"

"I don't drink alcohol very often. Is it okay if I have an orange juice?"

"If that's what you want, of course. You don't mind if I have something a little stronger? I drink alcohol very often," I said with a smile and a realisation that it was a long time since I had wined and dined a young lady and I was still crap at it.

"I ordered a gin and tonic for myself and orange juice for Dintle and devoured half of my drink as soon as it arrived. Dintle had her head buried in the menu as I thought about what to say next. If you have to think about what to say then the conversation is hardly flowing. I felt awkward and I think she did too. So, working on the old adage 'if you don't know what to say, say nothing', that's what I did and buried my head in the menu too.

I finished my drink and ordered another, this time a large one. Dintle hadn't even sipped hers so there was little point in asking her if she wanted another. I took a large gulp of the second drink before realising I hadn't put any tonic in the glass, nearly gagged, and began to think the evening was a mistake. Order a main course only and then head home, this doesn't feel right, is was what I was thinking.

"Do you know what you are going to order?" she asked, raising her brown eyes to meet mine.

"Steak, I think. And you?"

"May I have a steak too?" she said.

"Of course you may, have whatever you want. The dinner is to say thank you for finding the house for me. Please relax and enjoy the evening. You deserve it."

"I will try to relax, but I feel pretty nervous. This is the first time I have been taken to dinner with anyone other than my family and to be here with someone like you is… Well it's… Oh I'm sorry, you must think I'm such a child and so immature. I didn't sleep at all last night because I was so worried about tonight and what you would think of me."

If this last statement had come from the mouth of a south London girl back home I would now have one hand over my mouth to hide my laughter and the other over my wallet wondering what was coming next. But I did neither here.

"I'm so sorry if I have made you feel uncomfortable. And the guys around here are crazy not to taking you out to dinner, or am I missing something?"

"Oh, you have not made me feel uncomfortable, it's just me. And I have never wanted to go out with anyone around here. But when you asked me, I was so thrilled. It just felt different. I met you and something happened. I am twenty-three years old and have never had this feeling. If you want to leave, I will understand. You must think me such a silly girl, but if I didn't say it I think I would explode. I am sorry, it should be me that goes. I have made a fool of myself."

I stretched across the table to take her hand.

"Dintle, you have not made a fool of yourself, that was the sweetest thing anyone has ever said. Come on, let's see if we can get through dinner because once you have experienced my terrible eating habits you may never want to go to dinner ever again."

Dintle took out her handkerchief, wiped her eyes and then gently blew her nose.

We talked throughout dinner, not even noticing what we were eating. She talked about her job, her mother and father, who was a foreman at the mine, and how she had never travelled outside of Kimberley or Johannesburg. I told her very little about myself and deflected her questions back as skilfully as I could.

We were the last to leave the restaurant, although I have no idea if earlier it was full or empty. We literally just talked and looked into each other's eyes all evening. Dintle was like a flower freshly blooming in the spring sunshine, while I felt like a black winter twine strangling whatever it came in contact with.

I took Dintle home in the car. She laid her head against my arm as I drove, trying concentrate on navigating the car and not the nearness of Dintle. When we stopped, we parted awkwardly without kissing or holding each other, and she thanked me endlessly for a wonderful evening. We agreed to meet in a few days' time, using Rodney as the go-between. She told me over dinner that the meaning of her name, Dintle, was beauty. The most accurate name to describe her, in mind and in body.

I went back to my hotel room, lay on the bed and thought about Dintle. I knew that I had to stop seeing her. My life was in tatters, I was on the run, possibly for murder or, if the twins survived, possibly to be murdered. My wife must hate me, the kids never see me and here am I starting a love affair with an innocent, beautiful twenty-three-year-old, behaving like two star-crossed lovers mainly because I can't keep my shirt-tail over my dick. Pathetic.

Mum called in the morning as promised and, boy, was I looking forward to this call.

"Hi, Mum," I said with as much enthusiasm as I could muster.

"I've been thinking," she said, skipping any pleasantries. "You need to get back here. You're no use wherever you are, skulking in a corner. As I see it, the Old Bill think this is a drug turf war, and they haven't got anything from the taxi driver who witnessed the incident. So, nobody has anything on you, for anything. You have a family and that brings responsibility. Come back to your family and sort yourself out," said Mum, spitting out the words like bullets from a gun.

"If either of the twins croak it, there will be a murder hunt and it will be more intensive than any of the detective work so far in this investigation," I said. "If they come out of the coma they can name names for the heist and who assaulted them. I am better off here and let's see what happens. Stay at the house for a while, Mum, and look after my family for me. I've got to go now, I'll call you in a few days. Keep your eyes and ears open for me. Tell Susie and the kids I love them. Love you too, Mum."

I ended the call before she had a chance to respond. I knew Mum could be persuasive. She was determined to get her own way once she was on a mission, but she didn't have a chance this time. She had, however, planted the seed about me going home and triggered the guilt factor of my responsibilities of being a husband and father. Maybe the call was more sixty/forty in her favour.

Rodney and I spent the next few days driving around the area looking at mines, open and closed, and talking to some of the workers using Rodney's translation skills. There was a strong gun culture amongst the middle classes. Even those going to business meetings would leave their guns at reception in the secure gun cabinets. The stories of robberies, burglaries and hijacks on the roads were plentiful. There are no excuses for these activities, but the poverty was there for all to see and desperation and survival must be a major factor. Certain areas were no-go areas, and I was pleased to have Rodney by my side, guiding me through or around such places.

My own no-go area, Dintle, was, according to Rodney, telling friends and family about the wonderful Englishman who had come into her life. Dintle wanted me to come to her house to meet her family. This was definitely not on my agenda and my excuse was that we were moving into the house and I had business to attend to.

We did, in fact, move into the house, which was wonderful. We had few things other than clothes, so it was a non-stressful exercise, and Rodney and I spent most of the day familiarising ourselves with the layout and reading whilst sunbathing on the veranda. Bliss.

The first morning at the house I was awoken by the doorbell. Dintle was standing on the doorstep clasping some fresh, scented wildflowers. She had a huge grin and welcomed us to our new home. She entered the house, bouncing as she walked, to find a vase to put the flowers in. Unsuccessful in her venture, she was not to be defeated and found two empty jars that were put to good effect. A woman's touch was in our home.

We talked about the house and the hotel where we had stayed until Rodney decided to find something to do in his bedroom and left us alone.

"I have missed you, Bubbles. I think about you all the time. Do you think about me?"

"Yes, I do, Dintle, but I worry that this isn't right. I am older than you, and you are so sweet, you deserve to find love for the first time with a boy who is the same age."

"But I want you, I don't care for younger boys. Please don't worry, this is so right, Bubbles. Just hold me and feel my love for you."

Dintle fell into my arms, pulled my head down and kissed me with such passion that I was certain she'd never kissed anyone before. We stayed in that position for what seemed like an eternity until she pulled away.

"Just how I imagined. Just how I dreamed it would be. Oh, Bubbles, I love you so much."

"But you don't know me, you don't know anything about me. We have only known each other a few days."

"What is to know? You are here with me, I know you love me too, I can see it in your eyes and feel it in your kiss. I don't care about anything other than you and me, right now. It is all about this moment in time. It only takes a moment to fall in love."

I pulled away. This was like a Mills and Boon book, only I was a lead character with a hard on you could hang a coat on. God give me some willpower.

Dintle's mobile rang to save the day. It was her office making sure I had moved into the house and, once she had confirmed, they requested her back in the office. As far as they were concerned, the deal was closed and it was time to move on to the next one.

Dintle said her goodbyes, kissed me on the lips and returned to work leaving me a little stunned at her outburst and with a huge erection.

Once he knew his cousin had left, Rodney returned to the living room. "Is everything okay, boss?" he said, sliding over the arm of the sofa and landing on the cushioned seat wearing his dirty jeans.

"It won't be okay if that cream sofa is marked by your jeans. You need some new clothes, Rodney, and those jeans need to be cleaned before they walk to the washing basket on their own."

"Sorry, boss," replied Rodney a little sheepishly.

"Come on, let's get you kitted out. Is there a shopping mall in town?"

"I would prefer to go to the sports shop and buy a tracksuit and some new trainers."

"Okay, you drive. I'll pay for them on the understanding that I choose. I couldn't walk around with you if you bought a shell tracksuit and a Manchester United shirt. We're not filming for Unicef requesting aid in a third world water famine commercial"

"I don't understand, boss" said a puzzled Rodney.

"It doesn't matter and stop calling me boss. Tell me something about your cousin. Why is she so needy? You know, clingy. She is a beautiful girl but tells me she hasn't been out with other boys. Is this true?"

"You need to speak with her. I don't know anything about it," said Rodney shaking his head vigorously.

"Know anything about what exactly?"

"It's not for me to say, Mr Bubbles. Please let's talk about something else."

"But I am asking you, Rodney. Is there a problem with your cousin?" I persisted.

"We will be at the sports shop soon. We don't have time to talk."

"Let's head to Jo'burg then. I want to buy some things as well, so let's go there and we can talk on the way. Pull over and I'll drive," I demanded, leaving Rodney no escape route from my questioning.

"So, where were we, Rodney? Dintle, that's it. You were telling me about her lack of boyfriends and you not knowing about anything. Come on, Rodney, speak up."

"Dintle's parents were having a party at their house, it was their anniversary. Lots of music and drinking. Everyone was having fun. It was around midnight and Dintle was tired. She asked her mum if she could go to bed. Her mum said of course, so Dintle said her goodnights and went to her room. My dad had had too much to drink and said he was going outside to get some fresh air. Nobody took much notice, but he didn't go upstairs, he went to Dintle's bedroom and raped her. She was just fifteen years old."

A quietness filled the car. Rodney had tears rolling down his face but continued after a minute of silence.

"Dintle's mum found my dad forcing himself on her. Her dad fought with my dad, breaking his nose and kicking him out of the house and down the street. We never saw him again. Mum brought us up as best she could and we moved to the township. Although it had nothing to do with my mum, Dintle's parents have never spoken to her or my family since that day."

"Oh, my God, I'm so sorry. I had no idea. I wouldn't have put you through reliving that terrible night had I realised what had happened," I said.

"Dintle has avoided boyfriends or any attention from men since then. She has been content with her job and her family. Until she met you, that is. It has been like an awakening, a rebirth. She seems to have escaped from the nightmare of that terrible night. You must never hurt her, she is too fragile. I have never seen her so happy," said an exhausted Rodney.

"I would never knowingly hurt her. But I have literally just met her and now I feel her future happiness rests solely with me."

We drove in silence all the way to Jo'burg and parked up the shopping mall in Sandton. I turned the engine off and looked at Rodney, putting my arm around his shoulders.

"I'm so sorry, Rodney, truly I am. Come on, let's get this clobber and make sure you don't look like Jimmy Saville in a tracksuit. I will look after Dintle and she will be fine, don't worry. And if you come across anyone here that you know, remember the story you told about why you left your job."

I had said to Rodney that I would look after Dintle, but at this precise moment I had no idea how and in what way. Still, it was a minor problem in comparison to the other problems surrounding me. The next major decision was deciding if I was too old to wear skinny jeans because that was planned as my next purchase, along with some tight-fitting shirts and t-shirts. Rodney was eyeing the South African national tracksuit so I kicked him up the arse and pointed towards the Nike section. Within the hour we were stopping for coffee, laden with bags of goodies. Rodney couldn't wait to wear his tracksuit and trainers, so his bags contained his old clothes. That took me back to my younger days buying shoes. I always left the shop wearing my new shoes and my old ones in the box. I wouldn't mind going back to being sixteen again. I would certainly make a few different decisions and live a less colourful life.

CHAPTER THIRTEEN
BHEKA

We arrived back at the house, which was called The Maples, feeling a little exhausted – from shopping and the drive, but mainly emotionally following Rodney's sad story involving Dintle and his father.

"Rodney, I've been thinking. You're still my driver and translator, but there is little work to fill your day, every day, so here's the thing. Tomorrow I want you to enrol in college for a course on tourism or hotel management, or something along those lines. You're not stupid. A crap driver, yes, but not stupid. Your English is good and Afrikaans is your first language, so that's one more language than I can speak, okay?"

"But my ongoing wages from you, my job. I have left my job at the hotel for you," said a wide-eyed Rodney.

"Rodney, you look like Mo Farah when you pull that face. Look, everything is the same, you are just being given the opportunity to advance yourself, to better yourself in a subject you have experience in and enjoy. So, what do you think?" I said with my eyes wide open, mimicking his face.

"Who is Mo Farah? Yes, I say yes. Whoopee!" yelped Rodney.

"Okay, good, go to the college tomorrow but for now make us both a cup of tea, Mo," I said. We both laughed although I am not sure, like many things I say to him, that he understood.

For the next three days Dintle telephoned me, having got my number from her files at work, and texted me continuously day and night. She pleaded with me to see her and to meet her family. As difficult as it was, I agreed and said if she gave me the address I would arrive at the stipulated time and date.

I missed my family and speaking to Susie and resolved to telephone in the morning – if she took the call, that is. But here in Kimberley I was showering and pulling on my new strides as the day had arrived to meet the new in-laws... Just joking, but that is how Dintle must have seen it. The white skinny fit shirt was a bit of a squeeze, but when fully dressed I was a cross between Max Wall and a member of a boy band. I do worry about myself sometimes.

It was her mum that greeted me at the doorstep, while Dintle's pretty face beamed with delight over her mum's shoulder. I gave her mum a bunch of flowers and was shown into the living room, where Dad stood solemn faced with a hand outstretched to shake mine or wring my neck, I wasn't sure yet. I planted in his other hand a litre bottle of the finest single malt whisky I could find whilst shopping in Sandton. That threw him, as his eyes were glued to the bottle. He must have known how much a bottle of this whisky costs.

I was ushered to *the* armchair as there was only one. It must have been Dad's as it was positioned five feet from the television. We passed some pleasantries and moved to the table to eat. The meal was roast chicken, mashed potatoes and sweetcorn followed by a homemade apple pie with ice cream. It was all delicious and the buttons on my skinny shirt and trousers were straining.

Dintle's dad was not much older than me and talked about his job a lot, with encouragement from me as I was genuinely interested. Mum fussed around the table bringing in plates of food and taking out empty ones. We didn't drink at the table but Mum encouraged Dad and I to try the whisky while Dintle helped her with the dishes. It was all going well. There had been no direct questions about my life and I had been as vague as ever about business and how long I would be in Kimberley.

Dad and I went outside with our drinks away from the girls, who were in the kitchen. He was first to speak.

"Dintle is a lovely girl, but a very fragile one whose heart could be broken very easily. We love her dearly and have possibly been overprotective with her, so we have to take some responsibility for her vulnerability. Dintle has only known you for two weeks, but we have noticed a massive change in her and I think we have you to thank for that."

At this point I decided to speak up before any more direct questions were levied at me.

"Sir, when I first met your daughter I was overcome with how beautiful and effervescent she is. There was a connection between us that I cannot deny. My problem is that I feel she may be in love with the idea of love and not so much in love with me. I am older than Dintle and have seen more of the world. There is no doubt that Dintle is a wonderful catch for the right man, and with your permission I would like to see more of her, but I am trying to curb her enthusiasm and take things very slowly. I assure you I would never hurt or mislead her to the point of her unhappiness. I would like you and your wife to encourage her to mix with friends of her own age and not be in such a hurry to look for happiness with someone she has just met and hardly knows. I don't mean to be in any way disrespectful towards you or your daughter in the words I say." I finished my monologue and waited his response.

"Thank God for that. We were so worried that we would be walking our daughter up the aisle within the month. Here, have a top up of this magnificent single malt."

He refilled my glass, put an arm around my shoulder and guided me back to the living room.

"This conversation goes no further than us... Sorry, I don't even know your name? I asked.

"Bheka. And yours is Bubbles?"

"Yes, it's just a nickname. It's because I had curly hair when I was younger."

"Well, now I know something that Dintle doesn't know, the origin of your nickname. Good," said Bheka, slapping me on the back. "Here, have another drink, Bubbles."

"No, thanks, it's full already. Save some so you can enjoy it yourself," I said as the girls re-entered the room. I finished most of my drink, thanked Mum for a great meal and told her how nice it was to have wonderful homemade food. I kissed Dintle gently on the cheek and said I would call her. I then turned to Dad and said, "Thank you, Bheka.

I enjoyed my evening and our chat. Could I ask one favour?"

"Ask away, Bubbles."

"If possible, could I come to the mine as your guest? I would be very interested in seeing your operation and understanding the day-to-day tasks you and your team perform."

"Yes, come on Wednesday at two o'clock, I have a meeting before then but I would be delighted to show you around."

"Thank you Bheka, until then… Goodnight all."

As I turned to leave I am sure I heard the girls' jaws hitting the floor, seeing stern-faced Dad change into the amiable person that I am sure he really was. It was a successful evening in more ways than one. I drove home to find Rodney waiting to quiz me about how things went. I told him that I had not said anything about what he had said in confidence, that the meal was lovely and his aunt was a good cook. I explained how his uncle Bheka was charming to me and that we were meeting at the mine on Wednesday for a tour. Rodney was flabbergasted that everything had gone so well. I suggested he visited his aunt and uncle. I pointed out that their beef is not with him and he should go. We then discussed why I was talking about 'beef not being with him' and, at this stage of conversation, I decided to turn into bed and bade goodnight to my untidy housemate.

That evening Dintle texted me to say how much Mum and Dad liked me and how much she loved me, and asked when we could we be together again. I stalled for time in a return text but wasn't sure how much longer I could put off the inevitable coming together of Dintle and me in a more physical way. In the morning I was planning to call Susie to see what type of reception I would receive, but Mum beat me to it.

The mobile rang. I was still in bed and a little sleepy.

"Hi, son, it's your mum."

"Hi, Mum, you okay?"

"Have you thought about what I said about coming home?" she said. Nothing like getting straight to the point I thought.

"Have you thought about what I said?" Two can play at this game.

"Right, listen up. The twins are out of their comas, one is brain dead and in a wheelchair. The other, Charlie, will eventually return to full fitness. So, nobody's dead, there's no murder hunt and the Old Bill will put it down to drug-related gangs fighting between themselves."

"And what about when Charlie opens his trap and puts us all in the frame. What then?" I said, sitting up in bed, totally awake now.

"He won't want more of the same. His best mate is dead and his brother is a cabbage in a wheelchair. He'll just want to be left alone. Come on, get home," she barked.

"Is Susie there? Can I speak with her?"

"I'll go and get her. I'm going to find out where you are and come and get you myself," she said as a final flurry.

"Hello?"

"Hello, my darling, how are you?"

"Not happy and not well. Are we finished, Bubbles? Is this it, the odd phone call every couple of months?

Where are you? Living the high life somewhere, I presume. Probably a room full of prostitutes. I am so unhappy, frightened and lonely," Susie sobbed

"I'm sorry, honey, I never meant to hurt you. I just had to get away. What do you mean not well? What's wrong?"

"Clinically depressed. That's not just unhappy, it's an illness you have driven me to. I am dosed up with tablets most of the time. I hate you but I want you back; the kids want you back. What's happened to our life?" Susie burst into an uncontrollable gut-wrenching sob and Mum grabbed the phone.

She shouted down it, "Get home, you little shit." Then she hung up.

My next call was to Michael.

"Hi, Michael, what's new?" I asked with as much cheer in my voice as I could muster.

"Not much, mate. Susie is struggling with you not being around. Francesca and I go round to yours as often as we can without being a pain. But Susie's mum and now your mum is over, so she has plenty of support with the kids and that. I took a decision and gave the taxi driver twenty thousand pounds and told him to go to Spain with his family, well, his old girl, and rent a place for six months. He was the only weak link in the chain and the only one originally being interviewed by the Old Bill so I thought it best to get him away," said Michael.

"You did the right thing. Did you hear about the twins?"

"No, what's happened?" he said.

"Well, Mum tells me they are both out of the coma. One is brain dead and the other one will recover."

"Oh, I wonder where she got that news from. I guess it's good that no one is dead. It was always the plan to put the frighteners on them so hopefully that's the last we will hear from them. I didn't call you earlier because, to be honest, it's all been very quiet," said Michael.

"Could you do a little digging to confirm that info on the twins. I don't want Mum making things up to get me home."

"Sure, Bubs, anything else?"

"Yeah, I may need you to come out here for a quick turnaround visit. Could you do that?"

"No problem, just let me know when," said Michael, who seemed more like his old self.

"Cheers, mate, I'll be in touch."

I was concerned about Susie and her health. Some father I was, I never even asked about the kids or to talk to them. What sort of an arsehole am I?

The days passed and it was soon Wednesday, the day I was scheduled to meet Bheka. I had not called home as I was awaiting confirmation about the twins. I wanted to speak to Susie to see how she was, but until I had news to tell her, such as I was coming home, I knew I would just distress her more.

Rodney had booked up a course at the local college on tourism, which got him out of the house and away from under my feet, but I was genuinely pleased for him. Dintle called me to say how excited she was that I was meeting her dad at the mine. She updated me on her news about work, that they were busy taking on more staff and that she had won employee of the month, mainly for my rental. Then finally, she asked if she could she come to the house one evening just to cuddle up on the sofa and watch TV together?

I explained that the following day after seeing her father I had to go to Jo'burg on business for a few days or more. I told her I was sorry and that we would be together soon. It was a lie, but a good lie, I felt. I have had a few dates in the past which started as a plan to cuddle up on the sofa and watch TV. I don't know if it's just me but those evenings always ended up with sex, more sex and stains on the sofa.

The meeting with Bheka was great. He showed me round the mine and he did 'a day in the life of': what his day consisted of from eight in the morning to six in the evening. He had one hundred and fifty people reporting to him and two lieutenants to monitor their output. The machinery used for the mining looked old to me and procedures were not automated, but I guess human labour was cheaper than streamlining an operation with robots and computerised systems. The blackboards in Bheka's large office were full of scribbled notes, reminders, rotas and actions.

A male secretary had his desk in the corner of the office, which was completely covered in paper. It seemed like organised chaos to me but there was no doubting that Bheka was the boss and people jumped when he gave an instruction. I sensed his years of experience earned him a great deal of respect from his team and, as I walked with Bheka around his domain, it seemed a happy workforce.

Bheka had worked at the mine when they were digging for diamonds, but most of the work centred around the 'tailings' – piles of waste rock from the mines that were producing around seven hundred and fifty thousand carats of diamonds a year. De Beers was selling off its mines as going concerns to protect the workforce, but Bheka said the uncertainty of a job was his men's major concern, despite De Beers' optimism. There was little other work for the people of Kimberley if the mines closed for good.

The time I spent with Bheka was great. He was a charming, honourable man and I liked him a lot. We didn't talk about his daughter, which suited me just fine. I took the details of his work and mobile numbers and thanked him for a great day. All I could think of was seven hundred and fifty thousand carats of diamonds a year. The engagement ring I bought Susie when I was a taxi driver had a half-carat diamond. What a cheapskate I must have been!

I returned home, called Michael on his mobile and asked him to fly to Jo'burg on the next available flight. Just a one-way fare for now as his stay might be two or three days, I couldn't be sure. He didn't have a problem with that and I said that either I or a driver would collect him from the airport. I told him not to book a hotel, just let me know what flight he would be on.

Next, I phoned Susie. I told her I was coming home but I just needed a few more days, maybe a week, to sort some things out. But I was definitely coming home and could she tell the kids and Mum. Susie cried and told me she loved me for the first time in a long while. I couldn't believe it had been three months since I scampered out of the house, met up with Michael and legged it to South Africa.

The lovely Dintle had not texted or called so I guess she thought I was in Jo'burg, which suited me just fine. I had not spent much time in my new home, but it was spectacular to wake in the morning to glorious sunshine and beautiful unfamiliar birdsong. I felt happy, I guess because I had decided to go home and Susie said she still loved me. The twins were not dead, which I was pleased about, and the Old Bill were still nowhere to be seen. I was living a charmed life.

CHAPTER FOURTEEN
TIME FOR CHANGE

Michael was arriving at the airport at midday, so with a thorough description of Michael and a board with his name on, Rodney waited to collect him and take him to the hotel where we originally stayed in Sandton. I was taking coffee in the foyer, watching the comings and goings of the people staying there, when they arrived. Rodney immediately returned to the car to wait as he didn't want to engage in conversation with his ex-colleagues. Michael looked well as he crossed the room to meet me. It was good to be in the company of someone from home.

"Hello, mate, good to see you," said Michael as he gave me a hug.

"Good to see you too. Journey okay, all good?"

"Yeah, no problem. Who was the driver who picked me up? He looked familiar... Shit driver!"

"That's Rodney. He worked behind the bar here at the hotel but he works for me now as a bit of a gopher. He's a good lad, but you're right, a shit driver. How are Susie and the kids?" I asked.

"Susie is much better now she knows you're coming home and the kids are adaptable to change so they miss you, but life just carries on for them. The news about the twins was confirmed, although still unsure how your mum came by it so quick. Do you want a coffee, Bubs? I've left my overnight bag in the boot of the car; will it be okay?" Michael asked looking around for Rodney, who probably suggested it be left there.

"Yeah, we'll be off in a tick, let's just have a quick coffee then we can make tracks."

"Are we staying in a different hotel then?" said a puzzled Michael.

"No, I've rented a gaff. We can all stay there."

We drank our coffee and Michael reassured me that things were quiet at home. No twins, no Old Bill and no complications, just my disastrous home life, which was totally my doing. We made our way to the car and I drove us back, describing the house to Michael with Rodney chipping in about how lovely it was. Michael was looking through the window observing the townships, but the view was mainly motorway. Soon, we arrived in Kimberley.

Michael loved the house. He didn't quite understand why I had a year's rental, or why Rodney was living there. But he took a shower and changed and the two of us took ourselves off to eat at a smart restaurant I had driven past but not eaten at before. We settled down to a bottle of South African red as we considered the extensive menu and proceeded to order two steaks, cooked medium, with salad and a side portion of chips. I could have guessed our choice before we sat down at the table.

"Mike, when you left your job, what were the main reasons? What was it that you hated so much?" I asked.

"The company politics, instigated by the bosses, who were insecure about their positions in the company. The tediousness of doing the same things every day without the opportunity to progress in an industry I enjoyed working in. I genuinely believed that I could manage the staff as opposed to boss them and build the business in a creative and innovative way," said Michael.

"You still carry a lot of passion for the diamond business. Tomorrow I would like you to meet a friend of mine who works for De Beers here in Kimberley. His name is Bheka and he's the operations director, I believe."

Michael immediately jumped in.

"I'm not looking for a job down a mine, thanks," he said as he folded his arms across his chest and turned his head to look out of the window.

"I'm not suggesting that. But what I know about mining or 'tailing' the piles of waste rock, compared to you and Bheka, you could write on the back of a postage stamp."

"I don't really know the intricacies of mining," said Michael.

"But Bheka does, and you know how to classify diamonds for carat, clarity and colour, how to take the product to market, how to put a team together and how to manage and sell in a creative and innovative way. You said so yourself."

"I don't know where you are heading with this, Bubs, I really don't."

"How about tomorrow you, me and Bheka go to a mine just outside Kimberley that is for sale. If you and Bheka like what you see and if the financials for the current business stack up, I know what figure they want for it and I'll buy it," I said.

"Buy it? Buy a diamond mine in South Africa?" said an astounded Michael.

"Yes, why not? That way my crooked money goes into something legitimate. I wouldn't be the first person in history to do that. You, Michael, will be my managing director and Bheka will be your man in charge of operations."

"What does Bheka say?"

"I haven't spoken to him yet, but tomorrow I will. He's been in the business since the days when this vast hole in the ground was being mined. He has a wealth of experience and knowledge, and the mine we're going to see is still producing diamonds, not just tailing. Keep an open mind, Michael, but what do you think?"

"It's exciting, frightening. I would need to bring the family out here and look at schools. Francesca will need to buy into it. Getting on with Bheka is paramount. Why are they selling the mine – has it dried out, is it unprofitable? What clients do they have and are they being squeezed on margins?" Michael was staring into space as all his questions tumbled out.

Our food was only half eaten as Michael continued to quiz me, but I didn't have the answers. One thing I did know, however, was that he was hooked on the bait and would not sleep much tonight as he ploughed through his one hundred and one questions. We managed two bottles of red, me half a bottle and Michael a bottle and a half of nervous drinking. I called Bheka and arranged for him to meet Michael and myself at ten a.m. the next day at my house to discuss a business opportunity. He agreed and amongst the small talk told me that Dintle had gone for a drink after work with the boss's son... Good news.

Michael emerged from his slumber looking a little baggy-eyed. Rodney had cooked scrambled eggs with bacon and completely redeemed himself of his bad driving. I called the mine that was for sale and requested an appointment that day. They agreed but insisted non-disclosure agreements would have to be signed to protect all interested parties. The location was in the Kimberley area and mining was only taking place on the surface, but the shafts were still in place for underground mining.

Bheka arrived at ten sharp and sat down with a coffee. Rodney didn't want to see his uncle and slid out the back way. I proceeded to have a similar discussion with Bheka about my plans and his involvement. He seemed more stunned that I possessed the money to buy and run the mine with the plant, manpower and overall operational costs. Unlike my chat with Michael, I emphasised the opportunity for work for the Kimberley people and stressed that he would be able to hand-pick his team. Gobsmacked was the best way of describing his reaction, and it crossed my mind that although up to this point he had been an ally and supporter to my uncommitted relationship with his daughter, now he knew about my wealth, he may rethink that.

We travelled together to the mine and spent the next five hours overseeing their operations and discussing their workforce, clients, turnover and profit. I said that my financial accountant would be in touch to review the books and that, at this stage, we were very interested. The mine had been on the market for a little over a year, so they were delighted in our interest. We bid our farewells and I promised to contact them shortly with details of the way forward after speaking to my business colleagues, Michael and Bheka.

We drove to a nearby hotel and requested a meeting room that we could use for a few hours. We had much to discuss, but the overall reaction from both my colleagues was positive. They could see huge improvements on the current working practices operationally for production and the way the business currently goes to market for sales.

I asked them both for separate business plans as to how they would like to see their side working, including any key staff who may need to be brought in, retention of existing staff and a go-to market plan with timescales. I would need their input on initial costs, ongoing costs and any future investment costs. By the time we had concluded these early discussions, we were ready for the champagne I had ordered, which was drunk with gusto amongst much back slapping and raucous laughter. We were on the brink of a fantastic new adventure, but I needed to get home and retrieve a marriage that meant more to me than anything else.

CHAPTER FIFTEEN
HOMEWARD-BOUND

The next day I started making plans to return home, travelling back with Michael. I left it with the mining company that I would review their financials and needed copies of the property deeds to clarify what land would be mine. I would return to South Africa in around ten days to continue our talks. I also needed details of their current workforce to pass to Bheka. Both Michael and Bheka had ten days to put together their business cases, and both had given me their confirmation that they were on board, even though we had not talked about their financial packages. I was really pleased with how things were going, but there were still some loose ends to tie up.

During our champagne session I asked Bheka if he would invite Rodney to his home for some of his wife's wonderful home-cooked food. Rodney was a good lad and would love to be accepted by his family as he was an innocent in whatever the family feud may have been about. It was unfair on him to feel outcast and unfair on Dintle not to grow up with her cousin and, ultimately, his family. Thankfully, Bheka agreed to have him over for dinner the next week, which I felt was a great first step and a magnanimous gesture by Bheka.

I decided not to make contact with Dintle in the hope that her new relationship with her boss's son might blossom into something special.

I left Rodney at the rented house with strict instructions not to crash the car, make a mess in the house or miss his first day at college. I also told him that he should start thinking about a place of his own. He had enough money and Dintle may have a one-bedroom apartment on her books that he could rent.

Michael and I arrived back in the UK at Heathrow after a direct flight from Jo'burg. We jumped in a cab to Blackheath wondering what type of reception I would receive when I got home. I hadn't even taken my front door key with me when I left, so there I was standing on the doorstep, ringing the bell. Susie opened the door and stood there aghast.

"Bubbles!" She screamed. "Oh, my God, Bubbles."

She flung her arms around my neck randomly, kissing my lips, forehead and neck. It was the welcome I had prayed for but never expected. With all the noise, the kids were the next to arrive, clinging to a leg each shouting, "Daddy, Daddy." Over Susie's shoulder I could see my mum, her arms folded leaning against a door frame.

"I suppose I should put the kettle on now his lordship is home," she said in a solemn tone. But then a smile filled her face and she ran to the door to join in the group hug.

We all sat around the kitchen table drinking tea and they played a guessing game as to where I had been. My littlest got the biggest laugh. She suggested Southend-on-Sea. The kids got presents, which I had bought in duty free. Mum got some perfume and Susie got a four-carat diamond ring that I had purchased at the mine. It was a bit crazy, really, when in a month or two's time I would own the diamond mine and all the diamonds in it, but that was a little too much information at this particular moment in time to share with the family. Mum was the first to spot the South African duty free bag. My days of lying to Susie were over, so I told them that I was safe and well in South Africa and Michael had kept me up to date on all the activities back home.

We packed everyone off to bed and Susie and I held hands as we kissed the kids goodnight and walked into our bedroom together. Home sweet home.

THE END